ISLINGTON

Please return this item on or before the last date stamped below or you may
be liable to overdue charges. To renew an item call the number below, or
access the online catalogue at www.islington ... s. You will need
your library membership number and PI...

'Sex is sex. It means nothing but a physical union between two people who find themselves turned on and in the same place at the same time.'

Her lips opened to form an O. Pink, full lips. He sucked in his own bottom lip and shifted. He liked to tease her. Her creamy white English skin always turned a delightful shade of pink when he teased her. But he hadn't noticed how full her lips were before.

'You really believe that, don't you? You really think sex is just sex?' Her eyes flashed.

'Yes. I really believe that.'

He knew the truth. Love didn't exist. Lust, mutual attraction—that was what he believed in. And lust had caused him absolutely no pain the last nine years so he was sticking with it.

'It's time you let it go, Faith. Find something else. Move on. You never know—you might find something you're really good at. Current affairs, maybe?'

'I'm really good at sex!'

Her voice rang out at the precise moment when everyone got off the phone and paused. Her eyes opened wide, horrified. She turned away and bustled with her things.

Dear Reader

I am a massive fan of British journalist Dawn O'Porter. She is brutally honest and wine-spittingly funny and I adore the fact that she immerses herself in the worlds she researches in order to be able to *really* take you on the ride with her.

As a journo myself, I know that the only way to get the best quotes, the most interesting stories or the rawest response is to *be there*. To walk with someone and talk to them face to face. To immerse yourself in their world and their mind and *feel* the story so you really understand it. So you know more than just the facts.

In this book, sex journalist Faith immerses herself in the world of love and sex and relationships to try and understand it. But it's not until she meets her new boss, Cash, that she discovers that falling in love is much like being a good journo. There's no peeking around the corner and whispering questions from afar. You have to cross one hand over the other, bend your knees and dive right in. That's the only way to feel it and the only way to understand it.

So now it's time for *you* to jump right in and fall in love with Cash and Faith!

I love hearing from readers, so be sure to email me at jenniferraeromance@gmail.com with your comments or questions about Faith and Cash or anything else.

Love

Jennifer Rae x

SEX, LIES & HER IMPOSSIBLE BOSS

BY
JENNIFER RAE

Jennifer Rae was raised on a farm in Australia by salt-of-the-earth farming parents. There were two career options for girls like her—become a teacher or a nurse. Rather disappointingly for her dear old dad, she became neither.

All she'd ever wanted to do was write, but she didn't have the confidence to share her stories with the world. So instead she forged a career in marketing and PR—after all, marketing and PR professionals are the greatest storytellers of our time!

But following an early mid-life crisis several years ago Jennifer decided to retrain and become a journalist. She rediscovered the joy of writing and became a freelance writer for some of Australia's leading lifestyle magazines. When she received a commission to interview a couple of romance-writers for a feature article Jennifer met two incredible Australian authors whose compelling stories and beautiful writing touched her cold, cynical heart.

Finally the characters who had been milling around Jennifer's head since her long years on the farm made sense. Jennifer realised romance was the genre she had to write.

So, with little more than a guidebook borrowed from the local library and a you-can-do-this attitude, Jennifer sat down to release her characters and write her first romance novel.

When she's not ferrying her three children to their various sports, musical endeavours and birthday parties, you can find Jennifer at the boxing gym, out to dinner with her friends or at home devouring books.

Jennifer has lived in New Orleans, London and Sydney, but now calls country New South Wales home.

Other Modern Tempted™ titles by Jennifer Rae:

CONFESSIONS OF A BAD BRIDESMAID

This and other titles by Jennifer Rae are available in eBook format from www.millsandboon.co.uk

To my sister Donna.

If you hadn't rescued me from that bank,
I'd never have written this book.

Thank you for that. And for making sure
I never had to do anything completely alone.

x

CHAPTER ONE

THE FIRST TIME her phone buzzed, Faith Harris was too busy taking photos of a burlesque dancer's pasties to notice. They were new. Bright red and covered in thousands of dollars' worth of diamonds. Betty Boom-Boom was very proud of them and swung them from side to side for effect as Faith pointed the camera.

'Hang on, Bets, I just have to get you in focus—slow down.' Betty stopped swinging as Faith's phone beeped again. This time Faith plucked it from her back pocket and impatiently read the message on the screen.

Answer your damn phone. CA

Faith winced. He'd been calling all morning. She knew what it was about. Which was why she hadn't answered any of his calls. Or his emails. But now he was angry and she wasn't sure she'd be able to ignore him any longer.

'Sorry, Bets. I've got to sort something out.' Faith let out a breath as she slung the camera around her neck and stared down at her phone.

Cash Anderson.

The wheatgerm in her smoothie. The run in her stocking. The one bar on her phone.

The man who annoyed her, stressed her out and did her head in more than anyone else.

Cash-freaking-Anderson.

Who was calling her to give her the boot. The man had

only been in the job for four weeks but so far he'd upset programming, annoyed advertising and turned the entire editing department into fruitcakes with his constant demands and changes. And now he had his sights set on her and her TV show, *Sexy Sydney*. A show she'd been building for two years. A show that had gained her a reputation for honest, thought-provoking journalism. A show that he now wanted to can.

Faith breathed in through her nose and out through her mouth. Calm. She needed to be calm. She remembered her yoga. Be a bee. She stuck her fingers in her ears, closed her eyes and hummed—just like Sri Sri Ravi had taught her.

'Mmm…' she hummed.

She was going to lose her job. She had no savings so she'd have to move out of her flat and then where would she go? She'd left most of her friends behind in England when she'd moved here to follow her dreams. She'd only managed to make a few friends here—her job had taken all her time these past two years.

'Mmm…'

She'd have to move home. With her mad mother and her disappointed father and her layabout brothers who teased her incessantly about her job.

'Mmm…'

Then she'd start drinking heavily. And take up smoking and adopt a load of stray cats. And she was allergic to cats so she'd probably end up wheezing and not being able to breathe from all the cigarettes and cats and she'd cark it and they wouldn't find her until her parents noticed a strange smell coming from her room.

'Mmm—bloody—mmm…!'

Then she'd be dead and Cash-freaking-Anderson would finally be happy.

She unplugged her fingers. Not helping. Sri Sri and his yoga were useless. As was avoiding this phone call. She dialled Cash's number and waited, her gut clenched, her neck tense.

'About bloody time. Where have you been? Where are you now?' his gruff voice boomed through the phone.

'I'm interviewing Betty Boom-Boom. I told you I'd be here all day.'

'Forget Betty Boom-Boom. I need you here.' Faith felt the hairs on the back of her neck stand on end. His tone was abrupt and demanding. She was reminded of the principal of her boarding school. Unrelenting. Harsh. A man who was incapable of understanding, even when a young girl was miles from home—scared, lonely and unable to fit in. That principal had told her to 'toughen up'. And she had—which was why she wasn't going to let this man push her around.

'I really can't. I have to get these photos—the crew want to come and shoot tomorrow and I need to do the sheets up.'

'Faith. I'll expect you back here in twenty minutes.' He hung up. Twenty minutes. Yet she was forty-five minutes away. She closed her eyes, sucked in a deep breath and wondered, not for the first time, what the hell she'd got herself into. Only a few short years ago her dreams had seemed so clear. International travel and journalistic awards. They were the only two dreams she'd held her whole life. Ever since she was seven and found herself alone and unable to make friends in a new school full of girls with strange accents who seemed to consider her the resident freak. Back in those days her thick northern country accent, wild hair and outrageous comments made her the butt of many jokes. She'd learned to be small, to disappear and she'd gone to a lot of trouble to develop the thick, tough layer that now surrounded her. A layer she'd need to reinforce to deal with the abrupt, plain-speaking man who was determined to ruin all her plans. The *Sexy Sydney* show was her baby. She'd dreamt it up when she got her first station job back in Newcastle but no TV station in England would run it. Everyone called her bonkers; they'd snickered behind her back. But that was two years ago and everything had changed since then. Her dreams had come true. Escape. Freedom. Recognition. Finally. After being made fun of for so long, she was finally getting on her feet and now Cash Anderson was trying to take it all away.

'I've gotta go, Bets.'

'It's not that gorgeous boss of yours again, is it?'

Faith groaned. There was no denying the man was handsome. You could cut a piece of cheesecake with his cheekbones. But looks meant nothing to her. This man was a hard-headed businessman who wanted to shut down everything that was good about the station and inflict his stupid 'cost-cutting' ideas on them all.

'It's the good-looking ones you have to watch, Bets. I'm pretty sure he's trying to shut my show down.'

'The bastard!' Faith preened at Betty's indignation on her behalf.

'Right? It's a good segment. Australia needs to know about this stuff.'

'Of course they do. We're artists, not strippers, and what we do is a valuable part of our culture.'

'Yes! Exactly. But he doesn't get that. Him and his prudish attitude. You know what he told me at the last editorial meeting?'

Betty held her eyes in satisfying fascination. 'He said that all a woman needs in the bedroom is a smile. A smile! As if that's all it takes. That man has no idea how much waxing and plucking and shaping and moisturising goes into making that "smile" look hot. No idea.'

'Men,' announced Betty with a sniff.

'Men,' agreed Faith.

If only this man didn't hold her fate in his hands. Then she'd find ignoring him so much easier. But he could no longer be ignored. She'd been summoned to the Devil's den and if she wasn't there in twenty minutes, he'd have his staff out to poke her with it.

* * *

The blood pumped furiously in Faith's ears. It rushed like a waterfall through her veins. Cash was flashing one of those unfair electric white smiles at her. One of those smiles some men possessed that lit up their face and crinkled their eyes, making them seem younger and slightly sexy, which tricked your stupid heart into thinking they could be trusted. Which he couldn't. Especially not with the big boss of Apex TV in the room.

'Faith's segment is popular, I know. But there are some other things I'd like to try,' purred Cash—his eyes still on her.

She met his gaze and jutted out her chin. She couldn't trust him one bit.

'Such as?' Gordon Grant was an over-tanned man in his sixties. His American accent was smooth and polished and he was so damn sparkly, he had a way of making everyone in the room feel dull and dowdy in comparison.

'Such as sport. I want to introduce a new show based on Australian sporting legends.'

Faith groaned then looked up quickly as she realised everyone had heard her.

'You don't agree, Miss Harris?' Gordon smiled, his teeth blinding her for a second. His eyes travelled over her face and down to her neck and landed right where the button on her shirt wouldn't stay done up. She lifted a hand to it and sat up.

'No, actually. I don't.' She glanced at Cash. He was frowning at her. 'I don't agree. There are enough sporting shows on television already.'

'Australians love sport. It's our culture.' Matty Harbinger—the station's sports reporter—spoke up. Faith always thought of a terrier dog when she looked at Matty. All big teeth with his tongue always hanging out. And he talked too fast. 'Sport is in our blood. Cricket, tennis, footy. We can't get enough.'

'Sex is what Australians can't get enough of, Matty. Studies show that Australians are more interested in sex than any other country. But that Australians are behind the US, the UK and most of Europe when it comes to sexual satisfaction.' She glanced at Cash, who was now throwing death daggers her way with his eyes. 'People in this country are more likely to want to try new things in the bedroom than anyone else, but less likely to actually do them.'

Cash raised an eyebrow at her. The way he stood there, looking at her, made the blood in her wrists pump faster and her palms sweat. Betty was right, he was handsome. And tall, and broad-shouldered. She'd heard he was an ex-national rugby player. The muscles that rippled in his back whenever he took his jacket off meant he was still working out like one. He was tall and lean and chiselled and perfect. Except for his left eye. His one imperfection where a little bit of green had crept into the perfect brown rims. Which she was now beating herself over the head for thinking of. Right now. When her career was on the line and everyone was looking at her as if she'd just sprouted a second nose.

'The Australian public need this show,' she ended, her voice higher than before. She cleared her throat and swivelled her eyes to Gordon, who was smiling at her. Although leering seemed a more apt description.

'Is that so?' He turned away and set his glossy looks onto Cash. 'Well, Anderson, Miss Harris here would know. She is the resident sexpert—or so they say.' He tittered at his joke. As did Matty and half the other people in the room. She knew what they thought of her. The oversexed girl who reported on fetishes, orgies and polyamorous marriages. She'd heard all the nicknames. Fellatio Faith. Horny Harris. But she knew what she was. A good reporter. A vital part of this organisation. A woman who wasn't afraid to talk about sex and relationships and love. And she wasn't ashamed of what she did. But she was sick of having to defend herself at every meeting she went to lately. The chair scraped on the polished wood as she stood.

'You're wrong about this, Cash. The Australian public want to know about sex and love and relationships and communication. They want to know how to save their marriage. They want to feel like they're not freaks and that they can explore their sexuality without feeling they're doing anything wrong. And they're sick of watching grown men play games with their balls!'

The room fell into an uncomfortable silence. Every eye was on her. Felicity—the producer of the breakfast programme—snorted and covered her mouth. Faith's chest heaved. Her breasts strained against her shirt as it lifted up and down. She let her eyes lift to Cash and he stood there watching her. His eyebrow still cocked, his expression unreadable. Then she felt the breeze as the next button on her shirt popped open and exposed her bra to the table. The one Betty had given her. The one with the bows on the nipples.

'Bloody hell!' she cried before tugging her shirt back together, taking one final look around and fleeing from the room.

CHAPTER TWO

WHEN HE WALKED up to her desk, Faith was packing her coffee mug into a brown box. He recognised the mug. It was covered in red kisses and was usually full of black tea. He wondered why she bothered to make it as she always had to tip it out when it went cold.

'What are you doing, Faith?'

'What does it look like I'm doing? I'm packing.'

He decided to bite. Faith had a tendency to make him do that. She never agreed with him. She fought him on everything. It should irritate him, but it didn't. Out of all the new employees he'd met in the last month it was Faith who interested him the most. She was smart and she told it as it was. And she never sucked up to him.

'Why?'

'Because I'm leaving. You obviously don't want me here. You don't get what I'm trying to do so I'm going to go somewhere where I'm understood. Where I'm appreciated.' Her eyes were glassy. She was emotional. Faith was the type of woman who wore her emotions like a pair of very high heels. She teetered around on them. Fell over them. They got in the way. Which was one of the reasons he was canning her segment. She'd lost her edge. She'd become too invested.

'I appreciate you, Faith.'

'No, you don't. You think what I do is pointless and stupid. Which is why you want to replace me with sport.'

His eyes flicked to her shirt. She'd found a pin or something to do it back up but he could still see the curve of her breasts. He remembered those bows and swallowed hard, bringing his eyes back up to hers. She suited her segment. Sexy Sydney. But she'd suit something else. Maybe the weather.

'I don't want you to leave, Faith. I'll find you something else. You're a good reporter.'

'What? Are you going to find me a position as the weather girl? Make me dye my hair blond and giggle as I point to a high westerly blowing right up my skirt?'

Cash resisted the urge to laugh. Faith was funny. And quick and clever and he wondered why the hell she didn't want to move on. Why she was so determined to stick to the sex show that just wasn't working.

He'd been trying to get more advertisers to support the programme but they were hesitant. The content veered from quirky and amusing to deep and heavy from week to week. He wondered who was helping her produce the show—he needed to look into that. Maybe it was a production problem. The real problem, he suspected, was that, like him, audiences were just not that interested in nonsense like love and relationships and the various types of dildos. Everyone knew love didn't really exist. Everyone except Faith, who thought it made a difference when couples perked up their sex life with handcuffs.

'I'm sure we can find you something else. Something you'd rather be doing.'

'What I want to do is this. My *Sexy Sydney* show. I've built up a following. People love my reports.' She could talk as fast as a used-car salesmen, he'd give her that. She was engaging; she made you actually start to believe the drivel she was spouting. Her show was—at times—brilliant. But lately the content was getting too heavy. She'd actually cried on camera last week when interviewing some sex workers. Too emotional. Admittedly, she did seem to have a huge following if the comments on their Facebook page was anything to go by. Most people she came in contact with seemed to be under her spell. But he wasn't most people.

'It's just sex, Faith.'

Her eyes burned into him. He hadn't noticed before but they weren't brown as he'd thought they were. They were very, very dark blue. An unusual colour that reminded him of the ocean out at the front of his apartment late at night. As the wind blew and the waves fell against the cliffs.

'There's no such thing as "just sex", Cash. Sex always means more than just sex.'

Cash's lip curled into a half-smile as he watched her determined face. Once upon a time he'd thought sex was more than just sex. When he was much younger. But now he knew better. Sex was just sex. His mind snapped back; he didn't want to even think about what else sex could be.

'No. Sex is sex. It's a physical union between two people who find themselves horny and in the same place at the same time.'

Her lips opened to form an O. Pink, full lips. He sucked in his bottom lip and shifted. He liked to tease her. Her creamy white English skin always turned a delightful shade of pink when he teased her. But he hadn't noticed how full her lips were before.

'You really believe that, don't you? You really think sex is just sex?' Her eyes flashed.

'Yes. I really believe that.' He knew the truth. Love didn't exist. Lust, mutual attraction—that was what he believed in. And lust had caused him absolutely no pain the last nine years so he was sticking with it. 'It's time you let it go, Faith. Find something else. Move on. You never know—you might find something you're really good at. Current affairs maybe?'

'I'm really good at sex!' Her voice rang out at the precise moment everyone got off the phone and paused. Her eyes opened wide, and she turned a shade of beetroot, horrified, as a couple of the jokers who were supposed to be working laughed.

She turned away and bustled with her things. Heat rose in his face. She'd have to learn to toughen up if she wanted to work in this industry. He'd suffered rejection, ridicule and censure every day and if she was going to survive, she'd have to stop blushing and fumbling every time she got embarrassed.

He didn't want her to give up. This station was riddled with idiots. That was why it was in trouble. That was why they'd called him back over here. Faith was one of the few he wanted to keep on. But she had to step up. He moved closer and decided it was time he made her step up. He didn't want her to give up, so he did the only thing he could do: threw her right in the deep end and watched to see if she could swim.

When Cash leaned down, his mouth was perilously close to Faith's earlobe. She breathed in. He smelled delicious. Heady, warm and sexy. When he finally spoke it came out deep and rough in the broad, abrasive accent he used when he was angry. 'As your station manager, I insist you prove that statement to me.' But he wasn't angry. He was…something else.

Faith's heart beat in her chest. Being this close was not something she was used to. And not just close to Cash. She actually didn't get this close to men in general. As a rule. Which was probably why her heart was pounding and a bead of sweat formed on her forehead. He'd find out. If he dug too deep—he'd realise her secret.

'That is sexual harassment, Mr Anderson.'

Cash stilled. His eyes flicked to hers. There was no smile present on his face any more. He moved back a little. She felt the coldness of his look as it swept over her face.

'If I wanted to sexually harass you, Harris, I'd do it properly. On top of my desk. With you screaming my name.'

His eyes went hard, which was helping to slow down Faith's rapid heartbeat. He was still too close. Way too close and she needed him to step back. And now he was suggesting doing something she hadn't done in so long. With anyone—let alone a tall, handsome, gruff man who was trying to get rid of her.

Everything in her body throbbed. This had gone too far. She had to leave. For no other reason than she was actually considering what it would feel like to have sex on the desk with Cash. Multiple times. Using every Kama Sutra position in the book. And possibly some that weren't even in there. One after the other after the other after the other…

Faith mentally shook her head and pursed her lips together. She was a professional. She knew what this was—a man using his sexuality to get what he wanted. She'd read about that. She'd also read that those types of men wouldn't take no for an answer. You had to show those types who was boss—apparently.

'If you had any idea what I actually did every day, Cash, you'd realise that what I do is valuable.' She lifted her chin and put on her poshest London accent, trying desperately not to broaden her vowels. 'You'd realise how important my segment is to the Australian people and to this station.'

'All right, then.' He finally stepped back.

'What?' Confused, she tried to meet his eyes but he'd taken them off her and was now undoing the buttons at his wrists. He started rolling up his sleeves, revealing a set of thick tanned forearms. Lined with slightly bulging veins, she noticed absently before dragging her eyes off them and back to his.

'Show me what you do. Show me how your work is relevant. Prove to me that sex is not just sex and I'll keep your show on.'

'Prove it to you?'

'Yes. Show me *Sexy Sydney*. Teach me what you know. Convert me and you can stay on.'

Convert him? The man who thought sex was just sex? The man who—at last count—had been connected with over twenty high-profile women since he'd arrived back onto Australian shores four weeks ago? That was impossible. But it was her only chance to stay. So she grabbed it.

'Fine. Be ready at six in the morning. I'll pick you up.'

'Great. Gives me time for my morning surf.' He smiled and for once that smile didn't make her feel like trusting him. This smile looked more like that of a great white shark. All interlocking white teeth, hungry for some flesh. The beating of war drums sounded deep in her gut. This battle would be to the death. The only way to keep her show and her dream alive was to win—and this time she'd have to go all the way.

CHAPTER THREE

SYDNEY LOOKED DIFFERENT at six a.m. Quiet. Coiled, like a spring waiting to be let go and bounce crazily all over the place. When Faith had moved here two years ago it had seemed so foreign and strange. Everything was bright and sunny and sparkling. The people smiled too much. People in Australia worked to live rather than lived to work. It took a lot of getting used to. Sometimes it irritated her. She sometimes wished people would be a little more serious—a bit more ambitious, more like her. But as the sun bounced from the waves of the water onto the ferries that took people from work to the bars and restaurants and clubs that surrounded the harbour, she could admit that Sydney was growing on her.

What she loved the most was that it was a place where anything went. Where nothing was taboo. Where you could see a man dressed as a woman kissing a man passionately on the street at nine a.m. It was so different from the small country village she grew up in and literally a world away from the stuffy boarding school where she'd lived for ten long years. Here, she seemed to blend in a little bit more. With all the other crazies.

Faith stopped her car. There were no spare spots so she double parked and got out, hitting Send on the text she'd written to Cash.

I'm here.

She could only see the back of his building. Apparently he lived at the very top. His view would be magnificent. It would reach out so far he'd be able to see where the world curved. Of course a man like Cash Anderson would live at the top. He'd probably spent his life looking down at people like her. Small-town nobodies with only a sliver of talent but a truckload of determination. He was one of those people who determined the fate of people like her. And, frankly, she was getting a little sick of being beholden to the whims of people like Cash Anderson.

She'd finally started to feel different. No longer the nobody she'd always been at home. Or worse—the wacko everyone laughed at. Her mother had actually laughed when she'd told her she was going to be a journalist. Her father had given one of his lectures and her brothers had just had another angle from which to make fun of her.

She had always been an outsider—at home, at school, at every job she'd had since leaving college four years ago. But here, in this strange place, her fascination with love and relationships and sex had found a home. She had fans in Australia. Actual fans. And not just weirdo men with worn-out rewind buttons on their remote controls. She'd received letters from women who thanked her for showing them how to revive their marriages. From young girls who said she was the reason they learned to respect their bodies and themselves and from men who were happy she was able to teach them how to please their girlfriends in ways they wouldn't have thought of themselves. Real people with real problems.

She was helping. She was important. For the first time in her life, she mattered. Which was why this show was so important to her. She needed to make it a success. She had to make sure it stayed on air. With this show—she was somebody and with this show, she'd never have to go back to being nobody.

Her phone beeped.

What are you wearing?

What was she wearing? Faith's cheeks heated. Perhaps he thought she was someone else. One of his harem of twenty women he'd apparently bedded. Just for sex. She decided Cash Anderson was a pig. A sexy pig, but a pig nonetheless. She texted back.

It's black and hot and covered in leather straps.

Triumph made her lips curl into a smile. He'd be disappointed when he got down here and it was just her in her T-shirt and jeans.

Your car is covered in leather straps? Who are you—Batman?

Faith paused. What? Her phone rang and she pushed the green button.

'I asked, "What are you driving?" Are you the yellow bug or the red clunker?'

'The red clunker. I thought you said what was I wearing…'

As it always did when Cash was involved, her skin turned a bright shade of beetroot. Lately, she'd found herself trying so hard to impress him in order to keep her job—she more often embarrassed herself in front of him.

'You're wearing something black, hot and leather? Now who's doing the harassing?' She heard his laugh as he approached. His hair was short on the sides but a little longer on top—thick and dark and shining in the sun. And his long legs were striding towards her. The wind blew his white button-up shirt back, emphasising the muscles in his chest. He looked more casual today. His shirt was untucked. He looked suntanned and relaxed and ever so slightly sexy.

Faith pushed her bottom lip between her teeth. She didn't

want to think of him as sexy. Not when he was the man intent on destroying any dream she'd ever had. Not when he was her boss. Definitely not when she hadn't had sex in too many years to remember and was so desperate she was almost considering jumping the homeless man that slept on the beach near her flat.

Sex was something Faith reported on, not something she practised regularly. She couldn't remember the last time she'd been intimate with anything that wasn't metallic or attached to her own hand. Actually—she could. But she didn't want to think about that right now.

Cash was smiling that annoyingly happy smile again. The one that made him look like an American college boy. All red-cheeked and arrogant and fresh from the football field... and the memories of just how long it had been kept knocking on her brain—like an insistent salesman.

'That's not leather,' he scolded. 'Or black.' His eyes travelled from her head to her toes and her body heated from his look. *Knock-knock.*

'I thought you sent that text to someone else.'

'Why would I send a text meant for someone else to your phone number?' He smiled and chuckled at her before opening the passenger-side door with a creak. 'Get in, Harris. We have work to do.'

She slid into the driver's seat, a little mortified that her joke had backfired. This wasn't how the day was supposed to go. She had a plan. A plan to show him that what she did was important and why sex was about more than just sex. But in order to do that, she was planning on exuding utter professionalism.

'You look nice.' His eyes flicked to hers before he looked out of the window. His comment made her eyebrows raise. She gunned the engine of her 'clunker', as he'd called it. She'd purchased the red 1975 Kingswood a few weeks after she'd arrived. Everyone in Australia had a car. The general population seemed to all start driving around the age of eight

and seemed so familiar with their vehicles they all named
their cars. Matty Harbinger's BMW was named Bruce. Although everyone called it Sebastian behind his back. Her red
clunker was called Red. Obviously. She wasn't great with
coming up with witty nicknames.

'What do you mean…nice?'

'Nice. Pleasant. Lovely.' She felt his eyes on her. 'Do you
need a dictionary?'

'What's wrong with what I'm wearing?'

Cash sighed. 'Nothing. I said you looked nice. Why do
you get so defensive with me, Harris? Why do you argue
with everything I say?'

'I don't do that.'

'You're doing it now.'

Did she do that? She hadn't noticed. It was just that everything he said was usually wrong.

'When you said I looked nice I just thought you meant…
something else.'

'What else could I possibly mean?'

'When you asked me what was I wearing you meant what
was I driving.'

'That was an autocorrect mistake on my phone. You're
just being difficult.'

She wasn't being difficult; she was trying to be professional. She needed to calm down and start again.

'I'm sorry, Cash. I just wasn't expecting you to say something…nice.'

'Why?'

'Because you never say anything nice.'

Cash stilled and Faith swore under her breath. Offend-
ing him wasn't professional either. If only she were better at
being professional. Faith remembered a report she'd done the
other week on getting what you want in the bedroom. Speak
softly. Be frank. Look your partner in the eye and ask them
their fantasies. If it worked for sex, maybe it would work in
this situation. Faith cleared her throat.

'Cash, I'd like to know what you want. How I can help you understand what it is I do.'

She felt his eyes on her and gripped the steering wheel. She remembered the way he often looked at her. Unblinking. Intent; as if he was reading her mind through her eyes. He had a way of throwing her off balance when he looked at her like that, but she was safe as long as she didn't look at him. And at the way he cocked his eyebrow at her.

'What I want?'

'Yes. I want to know what I can do to change your impression that what I do has no value.'

'No value?' He paused and Faith felt a trickle of sweat slide from the back of her neck into her shirt. Red had no air conditioning and it was close to forty degrees outside. 'I never said your show didn't have value. Some of the things you report on are obviously stories that need to be told. Your problem is you get too close. You want everyone to believe what you do—that love is the answer.'

She turned to him then, her cheeks heating again and her palms slipping from the steering wheel in response to his annoyingly patronising tone.

'That's not true.'

'Yes, it is. You invest too much emotionally. Journalists have to put distance between themselves and the issues they're reporting on. That's what creates objectivity.'

Faith bristled. She didn't need a lecture on objectivity. If only he knew how distant she was from the topics she reported on.

'Sometimes you have to get close. That's the only way you can get the truth.'

'Advertisers don't like close. They like light and fun.'

'But that's not what my viewers want. They want me to get close, to get involved. They want to know more.'

He paused, then let out a sigh. Not a huge sigh but a little exasperated puff. 'People are not interested in love and relationships and everything else you report on.'

She stole a glance at him then. Of course people were interested in that—hadn't he heard? Love made the world go round.

'What about my report on online dating? That show got more hits on our website than any other. I talked to dozens of people who found love online and another dozen who found nothing but perverts and deviants. The public needs to know about this stuff. And what about the report I did on body image and the way women were perceived differently depending on their body shape?'

Cash breathed in through his nose, flaring his nostrils slightly. Faith watched him, then watched the road, then turned back to him, determined to get an answer from him.

'Was that the one where you were naked?'

'Where I…? What?' Faith turned just in time to veer away from a woman crossing the street with her massive Alsatian. 'Yes. But that wasn't the point.'

She didn't turn back to him. She could feel him grinning at her.

'I got naked to show women they had nothing to be ashamed of about their bodies. And I wasn't completely naked—my intimate parts were covered in leaves.'

'Your "intimate parts"?'

'Yes. My intimate parts. You know—the ones you don't show people.'

'I enjoy showing my intimate parts to people.'

Faith pushed the mental image of Cash's 'intimate parts' out of her mind. Professional. Sparkling. Insightful. That was what she was supposed to be.

'I'm sure you do, but I like to keep my intimate parts private. I only show them to a selected few.'

'Really?' Faith still wasn't watching Cash, but had her eyes intent on the twisting turns of the narrow Sydney streets. But she could feel him prop his elbow up on the console and move a little closer. He smelled of the beach and of something she somehow knew was just him. 'How many "selected few" have been privy to a viewing of your "intimate parts", Faith?'

'How many?'

'Yes. How many?'

'As in…as in…a number?' she stuttered. This conversation was definitely not professional.

'Yes. A number.'

His breath was warm against her shoulder. She could feel it through the thin T-shirt she was wearing. Her skin prickled at the feel of it. His lips must be close to her skin if she could feel his breath. His tongue would only have to reach out a little to lick her skin…

Faith's body throbbed. Her pulse hummed. Her foot slid a little further down on the accelerator. Professional.

'I don't think my number is relevant.'

'I think it's very relevant. You are the self-confessed sex-pert around here. I'd like to know how much of an expert you are. I'd like to know about your personal experience with sex.'

Faith's tongue lay dry in her mouth. Her personal experience?

'I've had enough to know what I'm doing.'

'Is that right?'

The air was now stifling. Faith lifted a hand off the steering wheel to pump the old rolling handle of the window to get it down. She needed air. Fast.

'That's interesting. Because I'd like to know how much is "enough"? Was it just the one partner? Or are we talking double figures?'

Faith stayed silent as the air finally rushed in the window. It was humid and sticky but it was air and the blood rushing through her head eased. A little.

'Triple figures?'

'No!' Faith's emphatic answer surprised even her. 'No. And I'd rather not discuss that with you.'

'Why not?'

'Because you're my boss and it's not…professional.'

'Forget about that.' He waved a hand out of the window. 'The sun is shining, it's a beautiful day and right now I'm not your boss. We're just two people going for a drive. Enjoying each other's company. Just talking.'

The vinyl seats were sticking. Red was a big car but still Cash seemed too close to her. He took up too much space and too much air with his questions and his deep voice with its gravelly assurances. But she knew what he was doing—trying to get something out of her. Trying to get her to reveal something she didn't want to. She had been working as a journalist long enough to know those tricks when she heard them.

'My sex life is none of your business.'

'I disagree. Your sex life is everyone's business. Especially when you've made a career out of it. Which is what I find so interesting. Why are you so willing to talk about sex on camera but unwilling to discuss it in private? What's happened to you in the past that makes you think sex is more than just sex? And why do you get so fired up every time I talk about getting rid of your show?'

Definitely too close. 'I get fired up because the Australian people need my show.'

'No. No one is that honourable. People are only motivated by one of three things, Faith—fear, greed or lust. So what are you motivated by? Why is this show so important to you?'

Faith felt as if she were snagged on a thorny bush. Cash was asking her questions she didn't want to answer. He was saying things she didn't want to talk about but she couldn't sit there and say nothing.

'If I had to choose from one of those, I'd have to say greed. I want to be successful. I want to be an award-winning journalist. I want people to know who I am.'

Cash remained silent for a moment and she felt him studying her. She flicked her hair off her shoulder and tilted her chin. She didn't care what he thought of her.

'All right. I'll pretend that's your real answer. But why sex? Why love? Why relationships? Why not choose current affairs? Politics? Sports? They're the flashy subjects that win the awards.'

'I don't care about sports or politics.'

'But you care about sex and relationships.'

'Yes.'

'And love.'

Finally she turned to him and held his eyes with hers. 'Yes. Love. I care about love.' She wasn't ashamed. She did care about love. She cared about it; she thought about it— she wondered why she could never find it. Something caught hard in her throat. She twisted her bottom lip between her teeth and turned back to the road, enjoying the glare of the sun as it bounced off the bitumen.

'Love doesn't exist, Faith.'

He said it so quietly Faith wondered if she'd misheard him.

'Of course it does. Everyone falls in love at one time or another in their life.'

'That's lust. Love is different.'

'You've just disproven your own argument, Cash. If you know lust is different from love you obviously acknowledge that love exists.'

'Maybe.' He shrugged. 'For some people. But it never lasts, which is why I prefer lust.' A heavy ball formed in Faith's stomach. This was not going well. He was going to fire her if he only believed in lust. Her show was based around the fact that everyone at some point in their lives would fall in love. Silence settled thickly around them. Cash was looking out the window and Faith could feel her career and the only thing that mattered in her life slipping away as the seconds ticked past.

'We're meeting with a tantric sex consultant this morning.' Faith forced a smile onto her face, trying to dissipate the awkward atmosphere that had settled over them. She glanced at Cash. He was silent as he hung one arm on the car window.

'Tantric sex?' he said absently, glancing her way with a slight grimace. 'Sounds fascinating.'

She wanted to tell him it was. She wanted to explain how she'd been reading about how tantric sex could make sex a more intimate and intense experience. She wanted to give him the statistics on the rise of BSDM and she wanted to explain the benefits of the Jessica Rabbit vibrator over the previous year's model, The Rampant Rocket. But she didn't. He seemed distracted and she could feel herself losing him with every speed bump they went over in the road.

'Is something wrong, Cash? Do you have something against tantric sex?'

She heard the smile in his voice. 'No. Just thinking.'

'About?' She shifted the old car into third and it jumped a little as she rounded the corner.

'About you and your show. And about…' She felt it when his eyes left her face and he turned away. 'Never mind. Not your problem.'

He sounded distracted, and a little bit sad. Which made her pay attention. Cash never sounded sad. Mad? Yes. Cross? Absolutely. Frustrated, impatient, angry? Yes, yes, yes. Sad? Never.

'I'm sorry if I argued with you.'

He turned back to her then and she felt his intense look. 'You don't have to apologise for disagreeing with me. I like that you disagree with me. I like that you ask questions and don't let anyone walk all over you.'

'Then what's wrong?'

'You know why they sent me out here, don't you?'

'To manage the station?'

'To save the station. Things are not going well, Faith. I've been sent here to make cuts, to find ways to save money and increase revenue. I'm not here to be the big bad bully who ruins everyone's fun and squashes everyone's dreams.'

Faith knew the station hadn't done as well this year, but she hadn't realised it was that bad. 'My show is good, Cash. Moving it into prime time will attract more advertisers.'

'Your show will never go to prime time, Faith. Last week you had someone use a vibrator on herself. That's not prime-time TV. That would turn off our family viewers, not to mention our family advertisers.'

'You couldn't see anything. It was just the noise and the point was—'

'It doesn't matter what the point was. Sex isn't accept-able on mainstream TV. Sport is. It's not personal, Faith. It's business.'

Not personal? Losing her job was personal. Calling what she did unacceptable was personal. Making everything she'd achieved in the last two years out to be worthless was per-sonal.

'You have no intention of keeping my show on, do you? This is a waste of time, isn't it?' Faith pulled the car up with a screech. 'Because if that's it, then you should get out now.'

His eyes met hers and she felt them. Hot. Challenging.

'I made a promise to you, and I'm going to keep it. If you can convince me that sex is more than just sex—I'll keep your show on. I'll back you a hundred per cent. I'll work with you to make this into something we can take prime time. But if I walk away at the end of the week thinking sex is just sex, then you have to admit it's not going to work. You have to give up.'

Faith turned back to the road. She revved up the idling engine. The stakes were now higher than ever before. No more Miss Nice Guy. He wanted to know about sex? By the end of today Cash would be dripping in sex. Not literally, of course. But today was about teaching this man what it meant to want something so bad you'd kill for it.

CHAPTER FOUR

PATRICIA FELLOWS WAS the kind of woman that you expected to be inside her cosy family home baking cakes. She was round and jolly and constantly cracking dad jokes.

Cash glanced at Faith. If she thought he was going to sit in this woman's backyard and have her bring him to orgasm with her energies—she was mad. And he was done.

He'd been willing to humour Faith. He wasn't sure why. Perhaps it was the thought of her leaving. She was the only person he knew who could sit him down, shut him up and fascinate him for longer than two minutes. And he didn't want her to go.

But her show had to. It wasn't right for the station and it wasn't bringing in the advertising dollars it needed to stay feasible. But she was right—her ratings were good. The viewers did enjoy the show. His mind flickered over the options. Perhaps the production team needed some help with direction. Maybe it was the script that needed work.

Wait. No. He didn't want to keep the show on. He needed more advertising dollars. Sport. That was what brought in the big bucks. Cash twisted his neck from one side to another. Faith was trying to sell him something he didn't want to buy. From now on he was going to make a concerted effort to not listen to her.

'Golly, you're a handsome boy,' gushed the elderly woman brandishing an incredibly long red stick with tassels each end. Cash stepped back. He didn't know what she was planning on doing with that stick, nor did he have any intentions of finding out.

'This is my boss. Patricia, Cash Anderson.'

'Gosh, if I had a boss like that I'd come to work dressed in nothing but a pair of very tiny black panties every day.'

Right. This was uncomfortable. Especially as Patricia was now licking her lips as she looked at him. As if he were a particularly juicy set of BBQ ribs and she hadn't eaten in a week.

'I might just sit this out and watch.'

'No! No. We don't normally get ones who look like you here. You will be the star of the show!' Cash now knew how Hansel and Gretel must have felt.

'Actually, Cash is only here to observe,' said Faith firmly. She glanced at him and smiled. A playful smile he felt deep down. 'He's still learning.'

'Oh.' The disappointment was obvious in Patricia's tone. Her eyes turned frosty. 'Sit over there,' she demanded, waving her stick.

A few other people had started to arrive. Mostly middle-aged couples named Barry and Sharon who all seemed to know each other. Faith received a lot of handshakes and hugs and everyone seemed to know who she was. They were all fans of her show. She managed their gushing well, he thought. She answered their stupid questions, laughed at their awkward jokes. Then she stepped back as the session began.

'Tantra brings harmony to all parts of our lives,' began Patricia as she started handing out silk kaftans. The men and women in the circle seemed to know what to do and immediately start to strip off, replacing their clothes with the kaftans. Cash shifted his feet and tightened the grip on his folded arms. This wasn't what he signed up for. He had no interest in watching a few horny old men shake their willies about.

Faith leaned in. 'Don't worry. You won't see anything.'

He glanced at her. She moved a little closer, as if pressing her arm against his would reassure him, but he didn't feel reassured. He felt uncomfortable and now aware of the woman next to him. A woman who was making his life difficult at the moment by not agreeing to move on to something else and allowing him to shut down her show. It was what the station needed and he'd find her something else—he liked having her around. For once he didn't feel so numb.

Faith smiled. He noticed how bright her eyes were. Blue and a little sparkly in the sun. And her teeth; white and straight. She was gorgeous, too gorgeous. But a little bit bonkers. *Just don't listen to her,* he reminded himself.

'Tantra is about respecting and harmonising our bodies, our souls and our hearts.'

His attention was dragged back to the circle of people whom Patricia was now directing to sit next to their significant others—their arms touching—just as his was touching Faith's. He held steady. Faith was attractive and she had a great body. Why couldn't he touch just a little? They weren't at the office and nothing was ever going to happen between them. He'd told her in the car they were just two people enjoying the sunshine. What was the harm in thinking that for a few minutes? A few minutes' escape before he went back to the real world. Before he became numb again. He heard the twittering of birds in Patricia's garden and felt the warmth of the sun on the back of his neck and allowed his shoulders to relax a little.

'First, we start with pelvic floor muscle exercises. This strengthens the grip of your "yoni"—the part of a woman's body that makes her a sexual being,' explained Patricia as she wandered between the couples, her voice becoming softer. 'Making it more pleasurable for the man's sexual core—his "lingam".'

Nothing too weird yet. Most people had their eyes closed, a few were whispering to each other—but as their pelvic muscles were packed away safely behind their kaftans, Cash was happy to watch.

'Now it's time to turn to each other and tell each other what makes us happy.'

The couples started murmuring and Patricia looked up.

'You too, Faith. I've told you before you can't come if you're not going to join in.'

Faith's blue eyes swivelled to his. 'I'm sorry,' she whispered. 'But Patricia thinks I'll make everyone uncomfortable if I don't join in. I usually come alone to do my research but seeing as you're here…'

'It's fine. You can tell me what makes you happy.' Strangely there was a pull inside him that wondered what did make her happy. Faith was always busy, always running. She seemed to be searching for some kind of answer and he was beginning to wonder exactly what was the question.

'We should sit.' She sat cross-legged on the grass. Cash shifted his body down. Too many years of bone-crushing rugby meant there was no way in hell he'd be able to sit cross-legged, but he managed to prop one knee up and spread the other out before he realised he had her encased within his legs. She looked small sitting there. Her hair was down and curled around her shoulders and her light skin glowed in the sunshine. Something else pulled at him—but he ignored it. Not the time. Not the place. Definitely not the girl.

'So what makes you happy, Cash?'

'Patricia said you had to join in, not me.' Cash didn't want to talk. He had a tendency to be too honest sometimes and he wasn't about to let Faith in to anything going on in his head. She'd be shocked when she found out what he was really like.

'Go on, it won't hurt.' She smiled and Cash sighed, shifting on the hard ground. Why did everything have to be so difficult? There was a simple solution to his current programming issues. Can the sex show, rejig the breakfast news programme and introduce the new sports show. But he'd promised Faith he'd let her try and prove herself to him. Although he knew she wouldn't be able to change his mind. He knew all about his stubborn streak; it was why he was making more money than he'd imagined he ever could and heading towards the top of the TV game.

'What makes me happy? Surfing. Steak.' He looked into Faith's eyes. 'Silence.'

Faith's lips didn't smile, but her eyes did. Something about them held him steady, unblinking. They were such pretty eyes and she watched him so intently, as if she was trying to read his mind by looking inside his eyes. He shifted a little again and then felt her hands on his knees. The warmth of them made him still.

'Relax,' she said quietly, her voice dripping in that honey warmth he recognised. 'No one's judging you here.'

The sun on the back of his neck instantly burned. He rubbed at it. She was wrong. He was always being judged. Everyone was. That was just the way it went.

'I like quiet too,' Faith began, removing her hands from his knees. Relief ran through him and he rested his hands behind him, still watching her though. Watching her watch him. 'I like to sit and listen. You know?'

He didn't, but he liked to listen to her talk. Her accent was cute. Posh, but every now and again her lips would curl as she manoeuvred them around a word and a strange broad accent would creep in.

'I like to just listen to the wind or the sounds below my bedroom window and switch off. Pretend I'm a cat and I can just sit and watch, then slink away when I want—where no one will find me.'

'You want to be a cat?' How was it that she could always say something that surprised him?

She laughed, her eyes crinkling and her teeth flashing in the sunlight. 'Sometimes. How about you? Have you ever wanted to be anything else? Anyone else?'

Cash thought about that. He thought about his brother. Yes. For years he'd wanted to be someone else.

'No.'

'I wish I were as brave as you.' Faith's smile faltered, her eyes falling.

'I'm not brave.' He was a coward; he knew that, but no one else did. No one beyond his home town of Warra Creek anyway.

'Yes, you are. You say what you have to say. You do what you have to do. You don't worry about what anyone thinks of you or what might happen. You're fearless.'

He watched her as she spoke. Something about her had him transfixed. He shook it off. Anyone would like to hear someone talking about them like that. It was just his weak little ego wanting a boost, that was all—which was what had happened when he fell in love the last time. She'd boosted his ego. But that was nine years ago—his ego didn't need boosting any more. He didn't need anyone trying to make him feel better about himself. He didn't need anyone.

'I'd call that being pig-headed, not brave.'

Faith laughed and the change in her face was instant. The wide smile transformed her face and he felt something pull at his chest. How long had it been since he'd made a woman laugh? Not simper. Not flirt with him. But laugh, out loud in the sunshine.

'I think you might be right there. But still. I'd love to be myself and not worry about what anyone thinks. I'd love to be brave like that.'

She was still smiling and he supposed that was the reason he felt a smile pull across his own face. He supposed that was why he wanted to talk.

'You are brave, Faith. You travelled across the world to start up a show that could have made you a laughing stock. But you did it. And you're here now. Proving yourself, standing up to me.'

'Is that brave, or just foolish?'

'A little of both maybe. But you're doing it. You're not running away.' Not as he had.

'Thank you, Cash. I think that's the nicest thing anyone has ever said to me.'

Cash raised his eyebrows at her. 'That's the nicest thing anyone has ever said to you? You need to find some new friends.'

His joke didn't make her laugh. She broke her gaze and although her body didn't move he could feel her pulling away.

The murmuring of the other people and the sounds of the birds started to get louder. He shouldn't have said that. He had a habit of saying the first thing that popped into his head, a habit he'd found hard to break over the years, but usually he managed to achieve it. There was something about Faith, though, that made him want to talk. That made him think he could trust her. He should have known better.

Just when he thought Faith was going to get up and walk away from him, she leaned in again. 'People don't usually say nice things to me because I don't often give them a reason to.'

Cash stopped. What did that mean? He wanted to know more, he wanted to say more but he didn't dare. He might say something else to upset her and today—here in the sunshine with her sitting between his legs—he didn't want to upset her.

Patricia was coaching again. Telling everyone to move their bodies, welcome the light through their pelvis. The people in the circle started to move in strange ways, lifting their hips and opening their arms. He hoped Faith wasn't expecting him to do that. Not only would his body probably refuse but it all seemed a little stupid to him. This wasn't sex. This was a whole load of rubbish about feelings and emotions. Sex was about sex. Pleasure. Rock hard, pounding, sweaty pleasure. End of story.

'Tantric sex is all about deepening the connection you have with someone,' Faith murmured from her position on the grass. He didn't turn to face her. He wished she wouldn't use the words sex and deepening in the same sentence. Especially not with that voice she had. The one that dipped from high and sweet to low and throaty in seconds. 'It teaches you to make love rather than just have sex.'

'Why would you want to do that?' This time he did look at her. He met her gaze directly and let his words seep in. Again with the honesty. But this time she didn't fall back; she actually leaned in closer.

'Doesn't it feel good? To make love rather than just "have sex"?' The way she asked had him puzzled. She was looking at him intently as if waiting for an answer. But she already knew the answer to the question. Either way it felt good. That was why everyone did it. Over and over, generation after generation. Because it felt good. He wondered what it would feel like with Faith. Would it be fast and passionate or slow and sensual?

As his imagination started to take over Patricia started giving orders again and Cash was glad for the break in the atmosphere. He pulled his hands up from the grass and planted an elbow on his knee, avoiding Faith's eyes again. He was sure Faith was one of those women who mistook lust for love and always wanted more than a man was willing to give. He usually steered clear of women like Faith, preferring those with…simpler tastes. At least he did now. That way there was no danger of feeling anything he didn't want to.

The couples in the circle shoved and shifted, their knees cracking in the air while their ample tummies made difficult the manoeuvre Patricia was now asking them to make. Cash watched, bemused, from his spot on the grass for a moment before Patricia's voice rang out across the garden.

'Faith! I need you.' Faith jumped up suddenly and held out her hands.

'What do you need, Patricia? I'm all yours.' Her voice was high again, and she spoke a little too quickly.

'Straddle that friend of yours over there. I need an example.'

Cash stilled. Straddle him? Faith turned. She wasn't smiling.

'I can't do that, Patricia. He's my boss.'

'All the more reason. This technique will teach you to communicate better. You'll learn how to listen to what each other needs rather than just talking over the top of one another.'

Cash wondered what Faith would do. She looked nervous, unsure. Slowly and tentatively she moved closer.

'I've been ordered to straddle you,' she said with an embarrassed smile.

'No, sorry.' He looked around Faith to Patricia. 'I'm not dressed for straddling.'

'Nonsense. Get on top of him, Faith.'

Faith looked mortified and Cash felt guilty. About what he'd said earlier and about the fact that he'd made her do this. All she wanted to do was prove herself to him; he owed her a fair chance. 'Come on, Faith, you may as well hop on. What could it hurt?' She looked so frightened he had to do something to reassure her. He lifted his arms. 'I only bite if you're bad.'

CHAPTER FIVE

FAITH LAUGHED NERVOUSLY and moved to stand with one foot either side of his legs.

'Are you ready?' she asked, her voice high.

The jeans she had on were tight and they followed the curve of her hips and clung to her legs. Cash lifted his hands and placed them on the outside of her thighs.

'Ready,' he said, his eyes not leaving hers.

She started to lower herself, coming closer, and his eyes moved to her stomach where her T-shirt didn't quite meet her jeans, exposing a pale sliver of skin that made the hairs on his arms stand up. His hands slid higher and her hands eventually landed on his shoulders. He tensed and she moved them a little as if caressing his muscles. Everything on his body went hot. For a second he forgot where he was and that there were a dozen eyes on him. All he could feel was her softness and all he wanted was to feel her in his lap.

His eyes landed on hers as her breasts came into view. They moved down, past his forehead, past his nose and then his lips. Her nipples were standing to attention. He clenched his gut, bit his tongue and moved his hands to her hips, easing her onto his lap. Her hips fitted right into his hands. She felt right there. As if that was where she was meant to be and all he wanted to do was pull her down on top of him. Feel her warmth covering him. She moved further down until he could feel her hot breath on his forehead.

Then her eyes were level with his and she was sitting on him. Her eyes opened wide. She shifted. She felt it. He felt it. He wanted her to feel it. She shifted again, getting comfortable and her breathing hitched. Her eyes moved to his mouth and all he could feel was her and all he could think about was her. Sitting on his lap, her hands resting lightly on his shoulders, breathing heavily so close to him. His head thumped. His lap throbbed. She sucked in a breath and held it before her eyes moved to his. Electricity shot between them. Her eyes that were so dark yesterday were now lighter. Almost the colour of a blue summer sky. Beautiful eyes. He moved his hands up until he felt the curve of her breast touch the top of his thumb. She let out her breath and parted her lips and he let his hand still, right beneath her breast.

'Exhale, Cash, exhale!' Patricia was saying something but he couldn't hear it properly. All he could hear was Faith's breathing as it changed and became heavier.

'Exhale,' murmured Faith. 'She wants you to exhale. Into my mouth.'

'What?' His voice came out all croaky and deep. What was she saying?

'Breathe out,' she whispered. 'As I breathe in—you breathe out.' He breathed out, letting his breath go in between her parted lips, then she breathed out and he felt the rush of hot hair go into his own mouth. His other hand moved around to her back. She was only slim and his hand took up most of the space on her back. He pushed her closer to him, letting his hard shaft get more comfortable. He ran his fingers through the soft hair that ran down her back and breathed out again, keeping his eyes on her lips. She shivered beneath his hands. Something was happening. Something that should not be happening. Not here in Patricia's garden.

Definitely not with Faith.

Cash moved his legs. He could feel her warm against his erection. It felt incredible. Not just like a beautiful woman sitting in his lap but something else, something much more intimate. She breathed out again and he sucked in her air, wanting to feel her closer, wanting to draw those full lips closer. She shifted and he shifted to allow her to get more comfortable but right then her head snapped up as if waking up from a sleep. She let out a noise and jumped up quickly. So quickly her head hit the bottom of his jaw and he tasted blood as his tooth went through his lip.

'Damn!' He gritted his teeth.

'Cash! I'm so sorry. Oh no. You're bleeding!'

Cash lifted a hand and held his mouth. When he pulled his hand away it was full of blood. His lip throbbed.

Cash swore loudly.

'Oh, dear. Oh, no. Let me get you something to clean that up.' Patricia was close and she was fussing.

'It's all right. I'll live.' He got to his feet and wiped his chin. Blood was still pouring out. He swore again but this time he kept it to himself. He should have known. He should have remembered. *You don't lose your head or someone always winds up getting hurt.*

Patricia returned with a fistful of tissues and he pressed them to his mouth. His lip hurt, but his pride hurt more. She'd jumped up off him so quickly. As if she'd realised what she was doing and who she was with. For a second he'd thought Faith might have felt something, that there was actually something happening between them. But there wasn't. She was faking it. For Patricia. For the show. Pretending to like him to get her own way.

His jaw hurt. He was hot and sticky and humiliated and all he wanted to do was return to the office. Get back to work. That was where he should be, not out here in someone's garden thinking things he shouldn't and feeling things he had no right to.

'Are you all right?' Faith's voice was small and a little timid, which was unlike her. He didn't want her sympathy. He knew she was doing her best to convince him that sex was more than just sex so he'd let her keep her show. But he wasn't falling for that. Not again. Ever. 'Do you want to stay?' she asked.

No, he didn't. He was cut and bleeding and angry.

'I think we should go.' He didn't look at Faith. He didn't want to see her face. Disappointed her scheme hadn't worked. Desperately trying to make him get into all this to convince him to let her stay on. He reminded himself that this was work and Faith was an employee and that was all this was. He just wished his throbbing shaft would listen as it twitched in disappointment.

CHAPTER SIX

FAITH WATCHED AS Cash creaked open the car door and slipped into the seat. The tissues were red with his blood and drops had fallen onto his crisp white shirt. Cracking his jaw and making him bleed was definitely not professional. She gripped the steering wheel until her knuckles turned white.

'Cash, I'm so sorry.'

'Forget it,' his deep voice grumbled and her heart sank. This was not working. She'd got carried away back there. Sitting on his lap. She'd felt his hardness and got carried away. Thought something she shouldn't have thought. Of course he had a hard-on. There was a girl sitting on his lap. He was a normal red-blooded male. She wasn't anyone special. That hard-on wasn't for her.

But for a moment, when he was breathing into her mouth, she'd thought it was. She'd thought he felt it too. The buzz that fired her blood when his breath hit her skin. But then he'd moved and she'd realised he was uncomfortable and wanted her off. So she'd jumped off. And split his lip open.

Seduction had never been her strong point. When she was young, she'd always been the girl standing in the corner. Watching the others snogging on the dance floor. And when she'd finally built up the courage to go further…things hadn't gone well. Faith twisted her neck from side to side. Which was another reason she needed this job. She wasn't exactly honest with Cash earlier. She did want to be successful—that was true—but the reason she chose sex and relationships rather than current affairs was that it enabled her to learn about sex in a way she'd never be able to on her own. And she'd learned a lot.

Sometimes she thought she was ready to put those lessons into action. But now, whenever she actually met someone she thought she could like, they were more interested in inserting part A into slot B than allowing her to explore their body with her tongue. Which was exactly what she'd wanted to do with Cash five minutes ago. But now he was bleeding and angry and definitely not interested in her tongue.

'Do you want to go to the emergency room?'

'It's a split lip. I don't think we need to bother the surgeons.'

'You should have moved your head.'

'Me?' He stared at the side of her head and her cheeks heated. He was about to blow up. Tell her what a screw-up she was. Abuse her and tell her she was an idiot. But he didn't. He laughed. 'So it was my big head that got in the way?'

'Yes. I was just trying to get up.'

He laughed again. 'Well, I'm sorry for making you split my lip.'

She glanced at him, surprised. He wasn't cross, nor was he ignoring her. She smiled and turned back to the road. 'That's OK. Just don't do it again.'

He laughed again and took the tissues away from his lip. 'How does it look?' His lip was swollen and covered in blood.

'Fine. Can't even tell,' she said, pushing the stick shift into fourth as she hit the motorway.

They laughed again and started trying to impress each other with the most pathetic injury stories until Cash looked out of the window at the passing scenery. 'Where are we going?'

'Thornleigh.'

'Thornleigh? As in the burbs?'

'Yep. Housewives and private schools and swimming lessons. Sydney's BDSM heartland.'

'You're kidding?'

'No. It's where Miss Kitty lives. Her clients are some of the most well-known people in Sydney. High society. Celebrities, soap stars, footy players. Anyone with cash goes to Miss Kitty's parties.' Faith glanced at him. She wondered if Miss Kitty's world would be his scene.

'What happens at these parties?'

'I've only been to one. I've seen men being led around on dog collars and women whose butts were red raw from spanking.'

To be honest, she'd been a little frightened and mortified when she'd first visited Kitty, but if her show had taught her anything it was to open her mind and find the source of pleasure in every act.

'That doesn't sound very sexy.'

'It's not the action so much as the feeling. Of being dominated. Of dominating. Of being in control or out of control. Like I said—sex isn't always just sex.'

'Is this what you're into?' Cash asked her quietly. She felt his eyes on her and was glad her window was down. He seemed to be asking as if he were interested in her answer. As if he wanted to know. As if the mistake she'd made earlier didn't matter. As if he liked her anyway.

'I like to try and understand relationships. The idea of being dominated or dominating has a lot to do with what one needs outside the bedroom. Sex is a manifestation of our whole life. Our attitude towards it is shaped by our lives— the way we feel about ourselves, our fears, our pasts.'

He reached for the knobs of the radio and twisted, finding a station that was playing country music. Faith glanced at him—she didn't take him for a country-music fan.

'Sounds like you're reading way too much into it.' Cash stared ahead. 'In my experience, sex has nothing to do with how you feel and more to do with what you want. Which is usually power. Sex is about power. Who has it, who wants it. And once you have the power, you can make someone do anything you want.'

Faith's neck prickled and her mouth dried up. 'Is that what you do? Have sex with women to have power over them?'

She felt his eyes hot on her. She knew he was looking at her intently, in that way he always did.

'I have sex for pleasure. I don't let emotions play any part. No one gets hurt that way.'

'Someone always gets hurt.'

Cash didn't say any more; he just turned to look out of the window and they stayed in silence as the sound of Johnny Cash singing 'Ring of Fire' rang through the car.

Miss Kitty was in a bad mood. She'd had a load of cancellations. Apparently a competitor had opened up close by and was offering discounts.

'As if it's a supermarket!' Kitty had bright blue hair and black fingernails but other than that she didn't look too different from the other women walking the streets of the leafy northern suburb. She had on jeans and a long white top with colourful beads slung around her neck.

While they toured her seemingly suburban house, Cash asked her about being a submissive. He wanted to know what it meant and why anyone would want to submit to another. Faith almost laughed. Trust Cash to not understand submission. It was a question, however, that seemed to make Kitty bristle. 'It's men like you who make the best submissives, honey. Men who think they can control everything and everyone. Being a submissive is about being attentive. Being aware of the needs of your dom. Doing whatever they need whenever they need it. It makes you a better lover. A devoted lover. Which is the best kind.'

Faith watched Cash's face. He wasn't comfortable here. He wasn't comfortable in Kitty's dungeon. He wasn't interested in her pulleys and straps. He didn't even touch her collection of whips.

'Can we have a minute to look around ourselves?' Faith wondered if Miss Kitty would agree. She was mostly a private person but Faith had managed to gain her trust over the last few months. Kitty blinked and folded her arms.

'What about him?' She nodded towards Cash as if he weren't there.

Faith winked and met Kitty's suspicious stare.

'I'll take care of him.'

CHAPTER SEVEN

KITTY NODDED AND left, clicking the door shut quietly behind her. When she left, the room seemed darker and eerily quiet. Silence. That was what Cash had said he wanted, but as she turned to him he looked anything but comfortable.

'I think I've seen enough.' He unfolded his tightly wound arms and moved towards the door but Faith moved quicker. She laid a hand on his exposed forearm and felt his dark hairs tickle her palms.

'Wait, not yet.' She needed him to understand. She needed him to see what this was about and why people needed to know. 'Let's just take a little look around.'

In the little light they had down here, Cash looked taller, darker and angrier. Faith shivered. His scowl should have frightened her, but it didn't. It was making her feel soft and almost liquid. She let go of his skin and moved to the leather-covered massage table at the side of the room.

'This is the "whipping table",' she explained and he moved a little closer to inspect it.

'Sounds barbaric.'

'Nothing happens down here that you don't want to. There are rules to make sure everyone's safe.'

'Whipping someone for pleasure doesn't sound safe to me.'

His arms were twisted again and his face still hard. Faith's stomach flipped. She recognised the feeling. Desire. She'd felt it before. Plenty of times. It wasn't unusual to feel desire for a handsome man. But not her boss, not Cash. And not here.

She moved away from the table and to the cage that stood in the corner. It was big enough for two and when she'd come to Miss Kitty's party there were two scantily clad women inside, kissing and licking and working themselves up into a frenzy. Faith stepped in. It was a small space and she felt fear for a moment, before turning to meet the eyes of Cash, who was watching her. Who hadn't taken his eyes off her.

'Safety is about trust. When you trust someone, you let them do things you wouldn't normally,' she said as he stepped closer and watched her through the bars.

'It's very dangerous to trust someone,' Cash said, his eyes narrowing.

He moved closer to the door and placed his hands either side of the opening. His presence there made Faith's heart speed up. He still looked big and angry. Definitely not safe.

'If you don't trust anyone, you can never be yourself. Isn't that exhausting? Putting on a face? Trying to keep everyone at arm's length?' she asked.

'I am myself. I don't pretend to be anyone else.'

'But you're worried about trusting someone. Why?'

Faith watched a shadow fall across Cash's face. A shadow that made his eyes go dark and his lips clamp together. 'Has anyone ever told you that you ask too many questions?'

Faith stepped back as Cash finally stepped into the cage. It was only a small space. Just enough room for two. He wasn't touching her but she could feel the heat from his chest against hers.

'I'm a journalist. That's what I do.'

'A good journalist listens—they don't talk.' His voice had deepened dangerously and Faith felt it vibrate around her. He filled the space with his body and his heat and his voice. Faith felt a little overwhelmed by it, by him. Something was happening as she stood watching him. Here in this dark space she felt less like herself. Bolder. Braver and a little out of control. She lifted her hands to grip the bars on either side of her and tilted her chin.

'I'm listening now.' His face was inches from hers, his dark eyes intent on hers, not moving—not even to watch her talk. He was looking into her and something warm and a little reckless washed over her. Trust. She trusted him. Carefully she moved her hands and splayed them across his chest. It was hard and tense. She shifted her fingers, massaging—trying to loosen him up, relax him. She wanted him to melt a little, as she was.

'Are you?' he asked, his voice gruff. 'Are you really listening to me?'

Her hands moved up slowly until they reached his neck. She felt as if she were somewhere else. This place with its implements of pain and atmosphere of isolation was making her heart beat harder. She wanted to touch him; she wanted to know what he felt like. The hard bristles on his neck rubbed against her palms and she felt it all the way to her toes. His eyes. Dark. Soft. She didn't see anything else. Just his eyes.

'Sometimes people don't always say what they mean,' she murmured as the breath in her chest got heavier. She could feel her breasts lifting and falling as her hand inched closer to his mouth. He wasn't stopping her and she just wanted to touch his lip—that was all. Nothing more.

His eyes hit her and she knew what he was feeling. His lids were hooded and she felt the heat of his desire as his body became even harder. Then she touched his soft lip with her thumb and all sense left her head. Desire turned into something else. Something much more desperate and she lifted herself up on her toes, anticipating and dreading the feeling of his soft lips at the same time.

The touch was fleeting. Nothing more than a brush, but a brush Faith felt buzz all the way through her body. She moved away, chancing a glance at his eyes. They were slowly opening as if he'd had them closed when her lips met his.

She didn't know what to say; she couldn't gather enough thoughts in her head to be able to come up with a reasonable sentence about how she was feeling so she lifted herself again to press her lips softly against his again before she could stop herself.

But there was nothing soft about his reaction. He pushed closer until she had her back against the bars. A small gasp escaped her lips and for a second, just one tiny second, she thought about pushing him away because for one fleeting moment she knew this wouldn't end well—but then the hotness of his breath met her swollen lips and she couldn't think of anything else but him. His heat and his hardness and the way he reacted when she flicked her tongue against his lips. His big hands gripped her wrists and pinned them hard against the bars. He pushed his hips in hard and she felt him, big and strong and angry.

'Where did you learn to kiss like that?' he growled and she let a tiny triumphant smile sneak over her lips.

She was in control here. He wanted her; she could taste it. That power made her head swell. She couldn't move her hands so she pushed her head. She didn't know where that kiss had come from; she'd certainly never kissed anyone else like that but it was as if she knew him. Knew what he wanted, as if he was showing her by the way he moved against her. It just felt right.

'There's a lot about me that you don't know,' she said quietly, letting her eyes fall to his lips. He reacted immediately, kissing her with a violence she'd never felt from anyone before. His hands gripped her wrists and his teeth clamped down onto her lip—a little too hard. But she liked it. She wanted more. She pushed her chest into his, letting the moan of pleasure fall from her mouth and he responded by sliding his tongue over her lips and finally…finally kissing her properly. Deep and sensual.

Faith's mind raced and her body pounded. She'd never been kissed like this. Never. Not even that time…but she didn't want to think about that time. She wanted to think about this. Him. Here. Kissing her, needing her, wanting her. A primal response to his own obvious desire.

Her eyes started to close and her mind drifted but when she felt the large hands around her wrists release, her mind came crashing back down to earth with a thump.

'You put your trust in the wrong people, Faith.'

Her eyes flew open. He'd pulled away.

'No, I trust you.' She felt drunk on his kisses and leaned forward, eager to feel his lips on hers again, but he pulled his head back, away from her—away from her lips. His eyes weren't soft any more; they were hard and she realised he was rejecting her. The drunk feeling that had come over her as he was kissing her vanished. Embarrassment replaced it as she watched him, staring at her, then as the seconds passed anger flashed through her, making her tense. 'You feel it too. I know you do. Why won't you kiss me?'

'I don't want to kiss you.'

'That's a lie. I know you do. I can see it in your eyes. I know you want me as much as I want you. I could feel it.'

'I don't.'

Faith's heart started to beat harder. She heard him but she didn't believe him. She remembered the feel of his fingers as they had slid up her back earlier today and the way he'd run them through her hair, then the passionate way he'd held her still just now so he could kiss her. He'd wanted her; she could feel that he wanted her. She remembered the look in his eyes as they breathed into each other in Patricia's garden. There was something there, she knew it—she felt it—but he was saying something else. Something much more humiliating.

'You're scared. I can see that. But you don't have to be. You can trust me.'

Cash was silent. His eyes watched hers; then they flicked to her mouth, then back to her eyes. Holding them. For a beat. Then another.

'What if I'm not scared? What if I'm just not interested?'

Faith felt the cold trickle all over her. *Not interested.* He didn't feel the way she did. And she was trapped in a cage with him. She couldn't breathe properly. She wanted to get out. She wanted him to let her go, but he didn't. He was talking again right when she wanted him to shut up. 'I'm sorry, Faith. What you want is someone to love you and I told you I don't believe in love.'

'I… I…' That was exactly what she wanted. That was what everyone wanted. But right now, all she'd wanted was for him to kiss her again. A sweet release from the torture she'd been going through all day.

'I thought I could trust you. I thought you were nice.'

'Well, you were wrong. I'm not nice at all.' Finally he stepped back and Faith was able to push her way past him and out of the cage. With a shove of her shoulders she opened the door to the dungeon and pounded up the stairs and didn't stop until she was outside and taking great gulps of fresh air.

She walked around the small suburban garden breathing in the scent of spring in the air and lifting her face to the sun. *Brilliant.* Once again, she'd misjudged the situation. Once again, she'd put her faith into someone who didn't deserve it. Cash had a reputation. He'd been dismissive of her; he'd tried to fire her; he'd told her he didn't believe in love—yet she'd still trusted him. She'd seen something that wasn't there. After every mistake she'd ever made, she still believed she'd be able to recognise when someone actually liked her. But he hadn't. It was just sex.

CHAPTER EIGHT

COUNTRY MUSIC BLARED from the radio all the way back to Cash's house. Faith wanted to change it but she was afraid if she reached for the knob he'd reach at the same time and they'd touch and the awkwardness that now filled the car would become even more stifling.

As she pulled the car up Faith felt her whole body grow hot. He wasn't interested. That was what he'd said. Faith burned with humiliation.

'Faith, should we talk about what happened back there?'

'No.' She held up a hand before glancing at him with a quick, tight smile. 'No need. It's cool. I lost my head for a moment, but it's over. Finished. No need to talk.'

No, if she could help it she'd never speak to him again. They could email. Or text. But talking she didn't want to do.

'I'd like to talk.'

'Well, I wouldn't.' She gripped the steering wheel hard but tried to keep her face passive. She didn't want him to know how much his words had really cut her. She didn't want him to realise that he'd opened a wound she'd thought she'd stitched up years ago.

'What did you think of Miss Kitty's place?' Change the subject. That was the only thing she could do now. If he wouldn't get out of the car at least she could talk about something else. Something that didn't hurt so much. 'It's not for everyone.'

'It's not for me,' said Cash determinedly. 'Sex isn't about tricks and masks and bloody pulley systems. It's about two people. Naked. Alone.'

But not her. She wanted to know why he didn't believe in love and why he thought sex was just sex. And she wanted to know why he didn't want to kiss her. But she wasn't going to ask. He wasn't interested so neither was she.

She caught him turning to face her out of the corner of her eye and made an effort to keep her eyes on the road signs at the crossroad ahead of her. *No Entry. Stop.*

'I don't like games, Faith. I don't like lies. I prefer things to be a lot...simpler.'

'Sex isn't simple. I've told you that. It gets complicated.'

'Only if you let it.'

Faith felt sick. Sick that for a moment she'd thought he wanted her as much as she wanted him. Sick that she'd got it wrong and all her professionalism was now out of the window. Sick that she'd lost any power she'd ever had in this relationship.

'Maybe your problem with my show isn't about the sex. Maybe it's you. Have you ever thought of that?' Humiliation was giving way to anger. Faith gripped the wheel harder as her foot accidentally slipped onto the accelerator, gunning the engine into a roar.

'This isn't about me—it's about you and the fact that no advertisers want to support this stupid sex show of yours.'

'My show isn't stupid. What's stupid is your attitude. You have a problem with intimacy—that's why you have a problem with my show. You're just a scared little boy running from the lightning in a storm. Afraid you'll get hit. Afraid my show is convincing people that love exists when you want to convince everyone that it doesn't.'

'You want to know why I'm canning your show, Faith? Because you're too close. You get too involved. You want so much for love to be the answer you miss everything else. You miss the fact that sometimes people don't like you. Sometimes they just want to get laid.'

Faith held back the pathetic whimper that was in danger of falling from her lips. That was it. Exactly. She remembered the mistake she'd made vividly. Mr Turner was older and had seemed so lovely. Calm and patient and he'd made her feel as if she was special. He'd told her she was talented. She'd believed him. Trusted him. She'd wanted to have sex with him to show him that she cared for him.

But then everyone had found out and he hadn't defended her. He'd let everyone call her names and laugh. He'd let them kick her out. He hadn't said anything to her parents and she'd had to bear the brunt of their humiliation. Her father hadn't spoken to her for twelve months. Her brothers still called her the Turner's Tart whenever they saw her. The first article she ever wrote after she left school was about proving that sex could be about more than just sex. But Cash was right. Mr Turner had just wanted to get laid. And she'd been there. She could have been anyone. Faith concentrated on her breathing and stared into the sun, willing the tears back into her eyes.

Cash was still talking, oblivious to the wound he'd gouged open with his words. 'Getting rid of your show has nothing to do with me or what I feel. It's got to do with ratings and advertising dollars. End of story.'

Faith took a deep breath. Her heart was heavy but her mind was buzzing with heat and mortification. 'I feel sorry for you, Cash. You care more about making money than making good TV and you don't believe in love, which means you'll never feel the high of losing yourself completely to someone or the low of being betrayed by someone you love.'

'How do you know what I've felt?' His voice was a growl. A dangerously low one. A warning that skittered down her spine but she was too angry and too embarrassed to heed it.

'I know exactly what you feel. Nothing. You're one of those men who are happy to take but never want to give.

A selfish man who thinks he can determine how people think and how they feel just because that's what you want.' Faith wasn't running on logic now—she was trying to find as many words as she could to throw at him. Something to make him yell back. Something to make him feel something because as he sat there cool and calm she felt humiliated. Exposed. Left out. And that emotion fired her temper even higher.

A wailing country tune started to sing through the speakers and Faith reached for the knob of the old radio in the dash.

'And I hate country music!' she said with finality, hearing a small but albeit satisfying click as the radio turned off. With her heart pounding and her palms sweaty, she hoped she'd won. She hoped he knew she didn't care

'You don't hold the monopoly on being hurt, Faith. We've all been there. It's just that some of us learn to close the book and move on while you just want to keep searching for answers you'll never find.'

'Yes, I want answers! I want to know why. That's why I do this—I want to know why.'

'Why what?'

'Why…why…'

Faith's heartbeat was still high and her nails dug into her palms as she curled them around the steering wheel. Her heart hurt and her eyes stung.

'I want to know why you can't admit that you like me.'

'You want me to blow smoke and tell you I like you? Is that what this is about? Do you want me to lie and say that I wanted to kiss you back there? I don't do lies, Faith.'

'You're an awful man, Cash.'

'Why? Because I don't like you? Why do you care if I like you or not? Not everyone is going to like you, Faith. You need to deal with that.'

'No, because you pretended to give me a go. You made out you were willing to listen and prepared to learn but you weren't. You have a closed mind and a closed heart and that makes you a soulless person. A person who is incapable of being loved. No one could ever love you, Cash. You have a black empty soul and if you had your heart broken once—you deserved it.'

Faith stilled and so did Cash. She could feel his elbow freeze on the console next to her. Something about his complete silence made her mind seize. She'd hit him. She'd finally made him feel something. She'd wanted that—she'd needed him to feel something so she wasn't the only idiot who exposed themselves today, but it wasn't relief she felt course through her. It was something else. Guilt. Pain. There was an old scar there; she could feel it and she'd slit it open. She'd become the bully who pushed and pushed until someone else lay bleeding and crying in the dirt.

Cash took a deep breath then let it out. He turned to look out of the window.

'Maybe I did deserve it,' he said quietly.

Faith wanted to say something, apologise, ask him who had broken his heart, but she didn't. She was confused and hurt and wracked with guilt all at once and the emotions that she'd longed for him to feel now climbed up her throat and clung on, suffocating her with their fierce grip.

'I think it's best we leave this for now.' Cash reached for the door.

'No.' The familiar burning of having to fight clawed at her insides. She wasn't going to lose. Not again. Not this time. 'You said I had a week to prove to you that sex wasn't just sex. A week. And you're going to give me a week.' She kept her eyes on his. She wasn't turning away, no matter how much it hurt. No matter how her stomach felt as his eyes hit hers. She'd seen those eyes soft and loving. She knew he'd felt something when they'd kissed, but obviously he didn't want to feel it and she wasn't going to beg.

He looked away first, nodding. 'All right. A week.'

Cash was lucky to get the door shut before Faith put her foot down as far as it would go and made old Red roar as loud as his thirty-odd-year-old engine possibly could.

CHAPTER NINE

CASH SQUEEZED THE top of his nose between his finger and his thumb. Today had been a disaster. The meeting with Grant didn't go well. His budget had been slashed again, and Grant didn't like his ideas for the new breakfast format. He wanted to stick to their original plan of syndicating US shows. Which meant less local content. Which meant fewer viewers, fewer advertising dollars and ultimately an even tighter budget. He had two weeks to come up with something. Two weeks before Gordon Grant was back in town and expecting the new schedules.

'Here are the ratings you asked for.' Lesley knocked on his office door and tipped the papers onto the corner of his desk before walking back to the door.

'Oh, and Faith is waiting for you in the boardroom.'

Cash felt his whole body still. The blood stopped rushing through his veins for a few seconds before it pumped back with a rush.

'Right, thanks, Les.'

He'd been avoiding thinking about Faith for two whole days now. And for at least a few hours he'd succeeded. But the rest of the time his stomach twisted in anticipation. It was just a kiss, he told himself. A simple kiss. He'd kissed plenty of women before. It meant nothing. Most of the time he'd forgotten about it before he'd finished his morning coffee. But Faith's kiss was a little more unforgettable. The way she teased and taunted. The way she pulled back, then the way she bit his lip. A shaft of something hot and furious shot right into his groin. He swore at the screen and pushed some paper around.

He didn't want Faith. He didn't like Faith. He'd told her that and she'd reacted the way he'd thought she would. She'd got upset. She'd thought it meant more than it did. But it didn't. It didn't mean anything. And neither did her words. He wasn't scared; he just didn't want anything. She had no idea. Maybe his soul was black, but it was trusting people that had done that. Work never hurt. When he was working he was in control. He determined what people wanted to watch and he decided what shows were going to air. At work there was no emotion, no past hurt and no blue eyes burning into him, accusing him, making him feel lower than a snake's belly.

What he needed to do was to sort out the mess he was in and get on with his job. It was pure lust that came over them in that cage. And on Patricia's lawn. Nothing else. Just sex, as he'd been telling her. And if he gave in to his lust that was all it would be—just sex. And Faith wouldn't be able to accept that. Giving in to temptation with Faith wouldn't be worth the fallout—not when his first priority had to be getting the station back on track. That was the only way he could leave and get back to the US. Back where he belonged. Not here with old memories stirring him up and a dark-haired temptress making him want to do things he knew deep down he shouldn't do.

With a sigh he lifted himself out of the chair. He wanted to get today's meeting with Faith over with. Once he saw her in the cold light of day he was sure his feelings of lust would dissipate. Then he could get on with convincing her to drop her show and take on something else. Maybe not the weather. Maybe she'd like a spot on the rejigged breakfast programme. She'd make a great morning presenter. Perky, happy, funny. Cute accent and even cuter arse. Perfect.

'Good morning.' Her voice poured over him like warm coffee. He strode to the chair at the head of the table, shaking off the warmth as if it were particles of ice.

'Morning, Faith. What have you got for me this week?' He didn't look up; he stared at the folder he'd set down in front of him and started writing something on. He wasn't sure what.

'I want to do a show on the top seven sexual fantasies for women. We did an online survey and I'd like to hire some actors to act them out, interview some experts and find out why women are so hot for them.'

Cash swallowed hard. 'And who are you suggesting we get to advertise during the programme?'

Faith's smile faltered. 'Sorry?'

Her blue eyes were dark again and she had on another revealing top. He could see the hot-pink bra she had on underneath her black shirt. He made a mental note to ask Lesley if there was a uniform policy here. A high-cut-uniform policy.

'Advertise. We need advertising dollars to stay on air. Which of our leading advertisers will want to lend their name to the breaks of a show that involves whipping and gagging?'

Her smile disappeared and her breasts started to rise and fall as her breathing got heavier. He moved his eyes back up to hers.

'Advertising's not my problem.'

'Correct. It's mine. Which means the concept is no good. Think of something else.' Cash stood to go. His body was hard and his voice was becoming gruffer than he wanted. She had no idea what it took to run a station. She ran around watching people get it on and tying each other up. She knew nothing about business. The real world. What it took to stay in control. What he had to do to stay where he was—on top.

'Condom manufacturers, book publishers, lingerie companies…I could name any number of advertisers willing to lend their name to my show. And for the record, gagging and whipping don't make the top seven women's fantasies.'

He looked up. He knew he shouldn't have. Her eyes were now bright blue—like the sky again. Challenging. Hard and unbelievably sexy. His eyes flicked to her soft pouty lips. A rash of heat spread over his body, and everything on him went hard.

'Then what are the top seven fantasies?' He knew he shouldn't have asked that but after watching her lips for too long he wanted to hear the words come out of her mouth.

Faith hesitated for a beat. Her mouth clamped shut. Then she looked down at her notes, her cheeks pinking. 'You'll have to wait and see.'

Not this time. He was in control here, not her, and he had to keep it that way. If he didn't, he'd be stuck here even longer and his mother had already threatened twice to visit him if he didn't go home soon. 'I want to know what the programme involves before I'll approve it. And, Faith...'

She looked up and his heart pumped fiercely.

'This will be your last show.'

CHAPTER TEN

HE DIDN'T WAIT to see her face. He didn't want to see the disappointment in her eyes; he just wanted to get out of there and refuse to acknowledge the feeling that was spreading over him. The feeling of carelessly crushing other people's dreams.

'I'm going out, Les.' He didn't wait for Lesley to throw another problem at him; he just walked past her, rolling up his sleeves and unbuttoning his top button. It was criminal to make a man wear a suit in Sydney. He felt tied up. Choked. He slipped off his tie and rammed it into his pocket as he stepped into the lift and waited for it to take him to the bottom.

Cash rested his head against the cool mirror on the back of the lift and scratched at his neck. He unbuttoned another button on his shirt. It wasn't his fault. Faith's show couldn't work. It needed more advertising and as long as Faith insisted on making everything so personal he couldn't get any more. If she'd kept it light and fluffy—he'd be right. He thought he might even be able to sweet talk a cereal company to advertise then. But lately she'd been digging deeper. The interview she did with the hooker was the worst. Faith had scratched and dug and delved until she'd made the poor woman admit that it was love she wanted. Every time she took her clothes off for money she wished she had someone to tell her to put them back on. Faith had cried, the damn hooker had cried and the soft-drink company who'd signed up to a six-month contract had pulled out immediately. Why couldn't she just listen to him? Why wouldn't she just do what he wanted?

He closed his eyes for a fleeting second as he remembered her in the garden. Sitting on him. Shivering under his touch and breathing into his mouth. Making him think she wanted more. She wanted him. But she was just another woman pretending to give him what he wanted but all the while manipulating the situation to benefit herself. It was an act to get her show back on air; he knew that. Just like that kiss. An act. She didn't feel that. They barely knew each other—there was no way she felt all that she was pretending to feel. But her eyes. They looked so sincere. As if she weren't even thinking about the show—just him and her and what they were doing right then.

The lift landed awkwardly and the doors opened. Outside in the sun Cash walked. Walked and walked and tried to breathe, but it was hard in the city. His shoulders ached. For a moment he wished he were back on the farm. Where he could sit on the back of a ute in the middle of a paddock and think. No distractions, no people, no sounds except the far-off bleating of a lamb. Here in the city he was never alone. There was always someone wanting his time—his attention. But he'd been gone from the farm for nine years. He hadn't felt the pull to go back there in a long time. When he'd returned five years ago for his father's funeral he'd barely been back at the farm five days. Why would he? Charlie and Jess had the farm running better than he ever could.

Instead of heading to the harbour, Cash turned and headed for the park. It was the only place he knew where he could sit and let his head fall forward and pretend he wasn't in the city.

He'd run into Charlie and Jess a few times on his occasional visits to the farm. Charlie had grunted at him and he'd grunted at Charlie and their mother had given them a lecture. Never, not any of those times, did he speak to Jess.

Nor did she speak to him. Her eyes were only on Charlie. Charlie—the superstar. Charlie; who'd dug the farm out of some serious financial trouble, who'd charmed the banks into lending him more money and who everyone believed brought the rain down in the drought of ninety-eight by sheer force of will.

Everyone loved Charlie and it wasn't until Cash had started to play rugby that anyone had taken any notice of him. He'd even played for Australia for a couple of years—but of course as soon as Charlie had joined the team Cash had been back on the bench. It was that summer that he'd met Jess. Jess had stroked his boyish ego and made him feel as if there might be something about him that was better than Charlie. Until Charlie came home. Then it happened all over again.

But that was years ago and Cash hadn't thought about it in a long time. He'd never questioned his choices. Until Faith started asking questions about love and relationships and trust. Cash found a bench and sat, trying to forget. *'You have a closed mind and a closed heart and that makes you a soulless person. A person who is incapable of being loved. No one could ever love you, Cash.'*

Cash breathed out and opened his eyes. He'd told her he didn't want to kiss her to stop her thinking that she was able to manipulate him. That kiss was all about control. She wanted it but he wasn't going to let her have it. He was in charge here and he was just going to forget that kiss. That mind-blowing, incredibly erotic kiss that kept coming back to him at the more inconvenient times. Like right now.

But just as he had pushed Charlie and Jess and the farm and everything else out of his mind to concentrate on work, he would do the same to Faith. Forget about her and her low-cut tops and silky hair and her smile that lit up her face. Work hadn't let him down once in the past nine years. He'd worked his way to the top. He'd been the superstar. Everyone had listened to him and, for once, Charlie hadn't swooped in at the last minute to claim all the glory. Cash stood to leave. He had to get back to the office—the phone would be screaming by now.

As he walked Cash focused on the joggers as they bounced past him. He watched them run, wondering if they realised how stupid they looked in their neon clothes and over-priced shoes. Charlie would have laughed at them too. He would have made Cash laugh, pretending to jog all the way to the pub where he would have sat him down and told him to stop being an idiot and go and talk to Faith. Explain everything to her. Charlie had always helped calm him down and sort through things. But Charlie wasn't there. And soon, Faith would be gone too. He'd told her it was to be her last show. He'd made her feel like he used to feel—as if what she did wasn't important, as if she wasn't important. And instead of it making him feel like the man in charge—he was left feeling like the world's biggest jerk.

'He is the world's biggest jerk.' Faith was waiting for Betty Boom-Boom to put the final touches on her make-up.

'Maybe he's right, Faith. Maybe this stuff is too much for people. He does have a business to run.'

'Don't take his side!'

'I'm not.' Betty looked at her with her kohl-lined eyes. 'I'm just saying you don't know what else is happening in his life. Maybe he's getting pressure from the bigwigs. You never know what people are dealing with behind closed doors. It could be nothing to do with you.'

Faith folded her arms. No, he was just a jerk. A jerk who kissed like an X-rated dream. A jerk with deep brown eyes that seemed to search her soul, that seemed to see what was there and like her anyway. But he didn't like her.

'Why can't people just say what they mean? Why do you have to always figure out what's going on in their heads?'

'Because most of us have been hurt and are afraid of it happening again.'

'I can't imagine Cash Anderson ever being hurt. He's always in control. A master manipulator of people. That's why they called him back over here from the States—apparently he's the man who can make anyone do what he wants.'

'It seems odd, don't you think?' mused Betty, swiping her lips with bright red lipstick. 'He had such a successful career over there—probably earning squillions. Why would he come back here to fix this tiny little Australian station?'

'I don't know—maybe he'd run out of women in America.'

Betty laughed and swatted Faith with a feathered fan. 'I've never heard you so cynical before, Faith. You're usually the eternal optimist. Seeing the good in people. Trusting everyone.'

'I don't trust everyone.'

'Yes, you do. You're like a child sometimes—always expecting people to treat you the way you treat them. Always expecting everyone to try their best and do good things. You need to hang around here a bit more. Then you'd realise that some people are just not worth it.'

Faith considered Betty's words. She supposed she was a bit of an optimist. And she did like to be liked, but didn't everyone? She didn't want Cash to like her, though. After that kiss she'd spent hours thinking of him. Wondering if he was thinking of her. But when she'd seen him in the boardroom, she'd known he hadn't been thinking of her at all. All he thought about was advertising dollars and how much money he could make. He hadn't thought about her. So she was refusing to think about him.

Although stubbornly his face kept creeping into the corner of her mind. The words he spoke to her the other day sounded in her ears—'You are brave, Faith.' The way he breathed into her mouth during the tantric session, the feel of his hands on her back as they caressed her bones. The hardness of his chest as he pushed into her and the passionate way he held her wrists when they kissed, as if he'd never let her go. Her stomach swooped. Deep in her core she swelled. She shouldn't think about these things. She wouldn't.

'I'm going for a little wander, Bets—come and find me when you're ready.'

Faith didn't want to sit amongst the half-naked women and the idle chatter. She wanted to think. Think about how Betty said you never knew what was going on behind closed doors and think about how Cash could kiss her like that then tell her he didn't like her. Dismiss her, as if that kiss had been nothing. But to her it wasn't nothing. She'd felt as if she liked someone as much as they liked her, despite what he said. Faith couldn't ever remember that happening. In the beginning, she'd thought Mr Turner had liked her—he'd said he did. But he hadn't. He'd used her and she'd paid for her stupidity with shame, humiliation and expulsion. Since then she'd managed to keep her heart fairly safe. She only kissed men who liked her more than she liked them. That way she wouldn't get hurt. That way she could control how she felt.

When her phone rang it made her jump. One look at who was calling and her heart started to pound harder.

'I'm on a job,' she said without saying hello.

'Where are you? I need you to come back to the office. I have to bump your show forward—I want it on air tomorrow night. We have a gap.' Cash sounded impatient.

'I've barely started. I can't get it done by tomorrow.'

'I'll help you. What do you need? Matty's cricket special has gone pear-shaped and I need to fill the gap.'

Of course—because helping Matty out was more important than producing a quality show.

'I'm still researching, I haven't started taping yet.'

'No problem. Tell me who to call—I'll help you organise it.'

'My cameraman is busy with someone else. He won't be available till tomorrow.'

'Then I'll be your cameraman.'

'No.'

'I'm not asking, Faith.'

Faith clamped her jaw shut. She didn't want to talk to him. She didn't want to see him and she certainly didn't want him hanging around with a camera for the next twelve hours. But he was the boss, and she had to keep this job—so she had to let him help even though the words tasted sour coming out of her mouth. 'Call Miss Kitty. I'll meet you there in an hour.'

CHAPTER ELEVEN

MISS KITTY LET them back into the dungeon and closed the door. Faith had managed to track down two out-of-work actors to play the parts of this particular fantasy and she was glad they were there when Cash turned up.

He'd taken off his tie and rolled up his sleeves so his forearms were showing. Faith flicked her eyes to his golden skin. She remembered the feel of the veins in his arms under her fingers. Her palms tingled at the memory of his soft hairs brushing past her hand and the way his biceps tensed as she ran her hands over them. Right here. In this room. Faith stepped backwards, away from Cash, away from her memories and away from that damn cage that stood in the corner—leering at her, taunting her.

'OK, Kieran and Julie—over there,' she ordered as the two scantily clad actors moved to the red sofa in the corner. 'We'll just finish setting up the lighting then I want you, Kieran, to get on top of Julie and pin her arms down.'

Cash was silent as he busied himself with the lighting and set up the camera. He seemed to know what he was doing.

'Not your first time taping sex?' she asked, keen to get the upper hand by letting him know she definitely didn't have any butterflies when he looked at her.

'It is actually, but not my first time behind the camera. I started out as a cameraman.'

Faith stopped plumping the cushion. She hadn't known that. 'You did?'

'Yes, for the regional news in outback Queensland. A mate of mine was the reporter and he asked me to come and hold the camera one day. I liked it so I made it my job.'

'You lived in outback Queensland?' Cash was a city boy. Suits, slick hair, expensive shoes. She couldn't imagine him as a rough and ready outback cowboy. But then again, with his tanned forearms and his hair a little tousled... She squinted—imagining him on a horse. Maybe she could.

'My father owned a sheep station. I was planning to spend my life as a sheep farmer until...'

'Until you picked up a camera.'

'Yes.' His answer was short and he looked away. 'Until then.'

Faith knew he wasn't telling the truth. She could tell in the way his neck went stiff and he busied himself with the cords. There was something he wasn't telling her, but she refused to care what it was. He didn't even like her.

'Should we get on with this? We have another five to tape after this, don't we?' His impenetrable wall was back up.

'Yes, of course.' Faith turned back to Kieran, who was trying to manoeuvre himself on top of a bored-looking Julie.

'Now, Kieran, you have to look like you're in charge. This fantasy is all about domination. You are an alpha male—you want her to do everything you say.'

Kieran didn't look much like an alpha male. His physique was spot on, but his hair was too perfect and he looked awkward propped up on his hands over Julie.

'No, no—not like that. Julie, you have to look like you're into him. You need to be a little more animal, Kieran—bare your teeth.' Kieran moved his gums to show off a row of straight white, perfect teeth. He looked as if he were in a toothpaste commercial.

'No, not like that. Get up, Julie.' With visible relief, Julie extracted herself from Kieran's embrace and Faith took up her spot. She lay back on the pillow and lifted one leg to curl around Kieran's.

'You're a vampire, Kieran. You're about to bite my neck. You want to taste my blood. Feel the desire.'

Kieran's face screwed up and Faith thought he looked a little as if he were trying to pass wind.

'Tense your arms, hold my wrists, put your lips close to my neck. Wait.' This wasn't working. Faith lifted her hands to tousle Kieran's perfect hair. 'Better. Now hold me down.'

Kieran's grip was limp. So limp Faith's wrists slipped through it.

'No, Kieran. Harder.' Kieran let out a frustrated sigh.

'I don't get it.'

'Get out of the way.' Cash's voice was deep and gruff and before Faith could get up Cash had pushed Kieran out of the way and was on top of her.

'There's not much to get, Kieran. She's the most beautiful woman in the world.' His body was warm above her; he pushed his hips down until they were touching hers. Until they were hard against hers. Faith's breathing had stopped when Cash leapt on top of her. He was too close, too big and a little too real.

'She smells like honey and her lips are swollen—as if she can't wait to kiss you.' Faith's lips pulsed. He brought his face closer as his big hands encircled her wrists and pushed them down hard.

'You want her,' he growled. His breath was hot as it passed her face and moved down to her neck. Faith arched her neck a little, allowing him to move closer. It brought her breasts up to meet his chest and her nipples hardened at the feel of him, breathing in and out against her. 'But you can't have her.' His voice had become quieter and deeper. Faith could feel it vibrate through her.

'She is a woman who needs to be controlled. She wants you to show her you're the man. You're in charge.'

Cash pushed Faith's wrists harder into the sofa and the

movement made her let out a small noise. It brought Cash's eyes back to hers. There they were. Dark. Soft and beautiful. They stared into hers. She could see it. She could feel it. He had to be able to feel it this time. The slight curve to his lips vanished as they stared at each other for a heartbeat. 'She wants you to dominate her. She wants you to take responsibility.'

His voice was low and she suspected she was the only person in the room who heard it. But she was sure she was the only person in the room who felt it. Deep down in her stomach. Him being on top of her was doing things to her body and her mind. They were both melting. He was taking responsibility. He was helping her and something like relief made her body slump. She shifted a leg, curled it around him and he released her wrist to push her leg down again.

'Don't let her do anything. You're in charge. She does what you want.' His eyes didn't leave hers. The room heaved with tension; even Kieran and Julie remained silent. Faith didn't know what to do. She wanted to stay where she was. He was so strong and a little animalistic. Even more in charge than she'd ever seen him and despite the fact that she hated herself for it—it was turning her on.

'Run your fingers through her hair, make her think you're being gentle.' Cash's hands snaked through Faith's hair and her scalp tingled. 'Then show her who's in charge.' He gripped her hair and pulled gently. It didn't hurt, but Faith felt completely at his mercy. Right then he could do whatever he wanted to her and there was nothing she could do about it. And she didn't hate it.

But this wasn't her fantasy, she reminded herself. She hated being at the mercy of anyone; she hated needing anything from anyone. But when she looked into Cash's eyes she didn't see anything to fear there. She trusted him.

Which was what she'd done last time, she reminded herself, and look how that had ended up.

Faith struggled against Cash's hands. For a moment, she

knew he thought it was part of the act but when she gritted her teeth and told him to let her up he released her immediately. She slid out from underneath him.

'Then, when we're done,' she explained in her best director's voice, 'it's your turn to dominate him, Julie.' Faith shifted herself and pushed Cash between her thighs. Now she was astride him with his head propped up and able to see her clearly. He looked shocked.

Faith tightened the grip of her thighs on his torso; she felt the muscles there hard beneath her. Heat pulsed through her but she ignored it. She ran her hands up and over his chest, her eyes still connected to his, and was satisfied to feel him tense beneath her touch and see his eyes open a little wider. Good, she hoped he was uncomfortable.

'This time you're in charge and he has to do everything you say.' Faith slid her hands up Cash's broad shoulders and out to his wrists. She ignored the feeling of his muscles as they bulged underneath her hands. They were just muscles. When she met his palms, she expected him to stay still and tense but when her fingers met his they curled possessively around hers. Interlocking in a way that felt wrong but at the same time perfectly right. Faith pushed his hands down hard and squeezed, hoping to hurt him. 'His job is to worship you and your body. You have to make him focus on one thing. You.' Faith held his eyes steady. Every now and again his eyes would shift to her lips but she'd dip her head and make him look at her again.

'Tease him. Make him think you're going to give in.' Faith dipped her head and her lips mere millimetres from his. His hands gripped hers tighter and his breathing became slightly laboured. She shifted a little and felt his erection hard against her. His chest lifted and fell and his head shifted a little as if trying to get closer. She moved back, staying just out of reach. She was in charge here. She felt like a woman. A woman who had a man completely in her power and she liked it.

'Then take it away.' She sat up quickly and the air that had seemed so thick seconds ago suddenly cleared. Faith pulled her hands from his grip and swung her leg off Cash, who was still lying exactly where she'd left him.

'Do you get it now, Kieran?'

Faith didn't walk to the camera, she swaggered.

CHAPTER TWELVE

'THANKS FOR HELPING me back there,' said Faith. Kieran and Julie had packed up and left. They had only been able to stay for two hours and luckily they had all the footage they needed. Cash had even sweet-talked Kitty onto camera—heavily disguised, of course. Cash was curling up the cables and hauling heavy lights over his shoulder. Faith looked away. She remembered his strength when he pinned her wrists down. She wouldn't have been able to move if she'd wanted to. She should have been scared or intimidated, but she hadn't been. It had felt good not to think, to let someone else take charge for a change.

'You don't have to do all this on your own, you know,' he said as Faith picked up a roll of cables.

'Of course I do. If I didn't write it and research it and organise everything it wouldn't get done.'

Cash stopped what he was doing. 'You do all this on your own every time?'

'Yes.'

'I thought you had Veronica as your assistant.'

'No, she helps Matty. And the person they assigned to help me research left so I do it on my own.'

'Why didn't you say anything?'

Faith shrugged. She was used to working on her own. The people she'd had working with her over the last two years had often started out excited about being a part of her show until they'd found out how much hard work it was. Then they'd left. She'd always been left to do everything herself. 'I don't mind.'

'Faith, your show is a one-hour weekly. It's a huge thing to organise. You should have let me know. I would have fixed it.'

Faith looked up at him. She didn't like the way he looked at her. Unblinking. Challenging. It made her feel as if she owed him answers but she'd been doing things on her own too long to answer to anyone. 'My show is delivered on time and is high quality. I don't need any help.'

Faith started walking up the stairs. She didn't want Cash looking at her like that. She was perfectly capable of doing this on her own. She'd done everything else on her own—gone to boarding school on her own, put herself through journalism school on her own, got a job on her own, moved to Australia on her own. She'd never had anyone's help and she didn't need his now.

Cash followed her up as she headed for his car. It was a very old station wagon. One that looked as if it should be filled with surfboards. That surprised her. She'd taken Cash for more of a luxury-vehicle kind of guy. But between this and the revelation that he was a latent cowboy she realised she had no idea who Cash really was.

He loaded his things in the back, then relieved her of the cables and shoved them into a spare corner, but he didn't shut the window down—he sat on the end of the wagon and patted the seat next to him. Faith wanted to move on. They had five more fantasies to finish today. She didn't want to sit with Cash, especially not this close. She was trying her best to stay distant and professional but every second with him was making that harder and harder.

'Sit down, Faith. Relax. You worked hard this morning—you deserve a break.'

'I don't have time for a break. We have to get this finished to be on air tomorrow, remember?'

Cash reached up and tugged on her arm, pulling her close and making her sit. 'Sit. I want to talk. We have plenty of time for your other five fantasies.'

So Faith sat. Even though sitting so close to him was doing things to her skin and her stomach.

'Has anyone ever told you that you work too hard?' he asked, picking up a twig from the ground and snapping it with his fingers.

'No.'

He turned, surprised. 'No? Not your family? Not your friends? Don't they miss you when you're at work all the time?'

Faith didn't look at him. 'No.'

Cash sighed and tossed the twig before planting his hands on the steel seat either side of his thighs. Faith felt his fingers brush her thigh but she didn't move, she just held her breath.

'I'd miss you…if you were mine.' Faith snapped her neck around. 'I mean if you and I were…' Cash's sentence trailed off but his eyes didn't. They stayed stuck on hers. Hot. Desperate.

But he wasn't. Faith's chest beat heavily. He wasn't hot or desperate for her. She was reading too much into it…again. She had to turn away before she pushed herself forward and kissed him again. She leaned down and picked up a twig, trying to snap it as Cash had but it was too thick. Cash's fingers met hers and they were warm and big and it made Faith swallow. Hard.

'You have to get it in the right spot,' he said quietly, taking the twig and snapping it before handing it back. When his fingers met hers she looked up. He was watching her again. 'You don't have to do this all on your own, Faith. I'm here for you.'

Those words pierced her heart painfully. Faith stood quickly. Too quickly. Her head hit the top of the wagon and the sharp piece that held the lock.

'Owww,' she complained, grabbing her head and checking for blood. She was close to tears. Her head hurt and her heavy heart hurt. *I'm here for you.* Four words no one had ever said to her. This was just about work, but as the tears stung her eyes she couldn't help but feel the pain in her heart where the permanent break was creaking open even wider.

'Here, let me see.' He reached for her but she swatted him away.

'No! No. I don't need your help. I'm all right—I can do this on my own. You go back to doing what you were doing and I'll get on with…what I was doing. I don't need your help. I don't need you to be here for me.'

'Faith…' He moved closer, reaching for her head again, but she stepped back.

'I don't need your help.' Her head hurt like hell. Her lungs were struggling to breathe and if he said one more nice, considerate thing those tears that threatened the backs of her eyes were going to fall and she didn't want him to see her cry. *Never let them see you cry*—she'd learned that early on in her school life.

'Well, you have it anyway. If you need it. I'm here.' He smiled and Faith felt the first tear escape. *Don't cry,* she scolded. *Don't you dare cry.*

'With bandages or cameras or…anything else you need.' He said it so quietly, so tenderly, but he didn't move—he just watched her. 'I'm here.'

Faith couldn't take her eyes off him. She wanted to, but she couldn't. Something about the tone of his voice and the way he was looking at her—holding her steady—started to calm her. Her heart slowed and the ache in her head eased.

They stood like that for a few minutes. Breathing. Watching. Waiting. She wanted his eyes to hold her steady and right now it felt as if that were all that was holding her up. Faith lowered her hands from her head and realised her palms were sweating and her legs were shaking. There was something between them—surely even he couldn't deny that now? If she let him know what she was thinking though, she knew he'd run, so she just silently held his gaze steadily the way he was holding hers.

Then a kookaburra laughed loudly and Faith blinked.

He too seemed to come out of a daze and looked away, breaking their gaze and moving backwards.

'Where to now?' he asked gruffly, turning away to close the wagon and secure the lock.

Faith felt the disappointment in her stomach. The moment was gone. Whatever had happened was over. He was back to being her boss and she the last thing he was thinking of.

'The next fantasy is the schoolgirl fantasy.'

'Really?' He turned back. 'Women are into that?'

'Apparently. So the survey says.'

'Who conducted this survey?'

'We did. Online.'

'Must be right, then. Come on—off to the school.'

'No! We can't film schoolgirls! The fantasy is not about actual schoolgirls—it's about dressing up as a schoolgirl and having your man be the teacher and then you...' Faith stilled. She'd read this on the fantasy list and skipped over it. She didn't want to think about it, but now...she had to actually talk about it. On camera. And find someone to dress as a schoolgirl and someone to be the teacher. Kieran and Julie could only stay for two hours. They were out. Maybe she should skip this one.

'If we had to leave one out—I'd be happy for it to be this one.'

'No.' He hit his hand on the top of the wagon. 'If we're going to do this, we have to do it right. Now, where are we taping it?'

'I don't know.'

Faith had deliberately not thought about this one. Not dealt with this one; she'd hoped it would just go away.

Cash put his hands on his hips. 'It should be in a bedroom. And since Kieran and Julie had to go—you'll have to dress up.'

'Me? No. I don't want to dress up.'

'Come on, Faith, you're always wearing some crazy outfit for these shows.'

'Yes, but not this. This is different.'

'Different how?'

Different because it cut a little close to the bone.

'It just is.'

Cash moved closer. 'It's your last show, Faith. Don't you want to get this perfect?'

Faith lifted her chin. He was still adamant this was her last show. She was still adamant she could change his mind and she was a professional, after all. A professional who didn't let her past interrupt her present.

'OK. I'll do it. But where are we going to tape it?'

He grinned. 'I know the perfect place.'

CHAPTER THIRTEEN

THE VIEW FROM Cash's apartment was even more magnificent than Faith had imagined it would be. It was a huge, open-style flat—like the ones she often saw in luxury holiday magazines. It was furnished very sparsely with just a huge L-shaped sofa and an enormous TV attached to the wall. There was nothing else. No decoration. No pictures, no personal mementos, no mirrors. But that didn't seem to matter as the main living space was dominated by the panoramic view of the ocean.

It glowed turquoise except for the occasional drift of white that interrupted the blue as a wave curled.

'You like it?'

Faith jumped. Cash was closer than she expected. She could feel him at her back.

She shrugged. 'It's all right, if you're into that sort of thing.'

'And are you into that sort of thing?'

She didn't think she was. During the past two years she'd been in Australia she'd only been to the beach once, and that was for no longer than an hour. The trouble was she'd been so busy working on getting her show made she hadn't had time to enjoy the sunshine.

'What I'm into is getting this scene done. Where do you suggest we shoot?'

The lighting was perfect. Sunlight streamed in against the pale walls and gave everything the perfect pale glow.

'The bedroom.'

Faith stopped. Professional, she thought as she turned to meet Cash's eyes. A small smile spread across his lips. 'Isn't that where this teacher-student action usually happens?'

Actually in her experience it wasn't quite as romantic as that. More often than not it had happened in the teacher's car.

Faith's stomach roiled. 'Where can I get changed?'

She hadn't wanted to participate; she'd even tried to call some other actors she knew to come and put the outfit on, but no one was available at such short notice. She hadn't gone for the whole outfit—that would be way too hard. She'd just found a school dress at a second-hand shop on the way over here and was planning on pulling her long hair up into a ponytail. No long socks, no blazer, no tie.

Cash pointed the way to a bedroom with an en-suite bathroom. She quickly got out of her jeans and pulled on the dress. It was a little too small and pulled across her breasts but she managed to do the zip up. Faith stared at herself in the mirror. It looked nothing like the stuffy boarding-school uniform from her youth—this was a summer Australian-style dress—but it had the familiar checks and the royal blue colouring that made it seem close enough that Faith had to grip the sink.

'Are you sure you want to do this, Faith?' he'd asked as his fingers accidentally brushed hers when they'd reached for the radio together. He'd given her plenty of opportunity to back out. But his resistance had only made him seem more attractive. She thought if he just got to know her, then he'd want her. If he just kissed her—he'd want more. If they made love—he'd realise she was his.

'Faith, how're you doing in there? We're losing the light.'

Faith sucked in a big breath and stood tall. That was over seven years ago. It was time to get over it. Time to move on. Except every time since then it had been the same. She'd chased and they'd always seemed reluctant, then when she finally had managed to get them between the sheets—they'd taken off faster than a gazelle being chased by a lion. Not that it had happened very many times. Three to be exact. In total, four miserable events that resulted in humiliation, shame and none of the sexual satisfaction she kept featuring on her shows. The truth was—she was a fraud. She knew nothing about sex. Definitely nothing about good sex. And she had no idea if sex was just sex or if it could be more.

'Faith?'

But she was a professional and that was what this was all about. She had to know. She had to figure out what she was doing wrong because one day…one day she was going to have some mind-blowing sex and it would mean something and he would love her.

Faith pulled her hair into a ponytail, and gave herself one more hard look before swinging open the door to meet the waiting gaze of Cash on the other side.

Holy mother of all that was holy and bad.

Faith was dressed in a very tight, very short school dress and it was doing things to his body he was ashamed of. He'd never had a schoolgirl fantasy. Well, not since high school anyway, when the girls had all laughed at his long, lanky limbs and cowboy hat. Girls had only ever talked to him because of his superstar brother. But Faith looked different. Grown up. Sophisticated. A woman playing dress up. She was no innocent girl and it made his blood run faster and his brain start to curl.

'Well, how do I look?'

Hot. Forbidden. Dangerous. Sexy as hell.

'Fine,' he said and turned back to the camera.

Out of bounds, he told himself. An employee, he reminded himself as he tugged at the cords. Someone who will get too attached.

Back at Kitty's place, there had been a moment. A strange

moment where everything had seemed to disappear, and he'd started to think some stupid things. Like he could trust her. Like there was something about her that was different. Like she needed him. But he'd spent the forty-minute drive back to the city with the music blaring those thoughts out of his head.

Now here she was, in that short dress—looking innocent and vulnerable and in control and sexy all at once and he had an urge to throw her over his shoulder and take her away. An urge to help her. To stop her feeling as if she had to do this all on her own.

A strange layer of sadness settled on his shoulder. He knew what it felt like to think you had to do everything on your own. To prove that you didn't need anyone else. He shook the feeling off. What she did or didn't do was nothing to him. He couldn't trust her—he didn't know her. He was just confused right now by her short skirt and big blue innocent eyes. Any man would be confused, he said to himself. Any man would be having the thoughts he was having right now.

'Where do you want me?' she asked, all innocent professionalism.

Cash gritted his teeth. 'On the chair by the window.'

'Really? We're in the bedroom—I would have thought you wanted me on the bed.'

Cash let out a breath and watched as she flung herself onto his bed. The normally perfect cover rumpled and his whole body went hard. She had no shoes on and had curled her legs up but because the dress was so short, he could see her thighs and a hint of hot-pink panties.

'Hitch your skirt down—I can see your underwear.'

He turned away again and fiddled with some knobs he didn't need to fiddle with. He was enjoying being the cameraman again. It had been nearly ten years since he'd been behind a camera. Ten years since he'd made the decision to leave his small town and be someone else. And it had worked. He was someone else. Successful. Wealthy. Powerful. But as he turned the knobs way too hard he realised there was still a little bit of that country boy in him. That awkward country bloke who saw a pretty girl and lost all his sense.

'Lay back a little and I'll crop it in close before panning out.'

'Right.'

When he turned back Faith was strewn across the bed, her hands behind her head. He'd had plenty of women in his bed before but none had looked as inviting as this. None had made his body jump the way she did.

'You may be surprised to know that many women enjoy dressing up as a schoolgirl.' Faith's voice was a little wooden—it lacked the animation she usually brought to her programme. Cash moved his eyes from the camera and peered at her.

'What's up?'

'Nothing.' Her voice was tight, angry.

'Let's try again and this time try and act as if you're enjoying yourself.'

Faith started again. Her voice was better but the wrinkle between her eyes was still there. Frustrated, angry. She twisted her body to sit up and Cash thought he saw a flash of pink again but kept rolling, not trusting himself to take his hands off the camera and suspicious she wouldn't like him to stop her again.

'Some women enjoy playing the naughty tart who won't stop teasing you until you pull her over your knee and give her the spanking she craves. That's right: loads of grown women fantasise about getting a proper spanking from their man. A spanking from you is exciting for two reasons: not only does this mild show of dominance hurt so good, but it also usually leads straight into hot, hot sex.'

Her voice had slowed down. Her knees were up now and he could definitely see a flash of pink.

'We'll have to do it again—I can see your underwear.'

Annoyance flashed across Faith's face. 'Again? Once is bad enough in this outfit.'

Cash straightened his back. Her mouth had turned down and her cheeks were pink. She wasn't happy at all. 'Sometimes these things take a few takes.'

'I didn't even want one.'

Maybe he was putting too much pressure on her. He knew he had a tendency to do that. And he was particularly hard on Faith but after getting to know her a little more, he wasn't sure that was the right thing to do. She was usually so confident talking about sex, but today she was struggling.

'What is it about this fantasy you don't like?' he asked, curious about what had ruffled the feathers of Sydney's sexpert. Surely a little role playing didn't make her this uncomfortable. She'd been more than comfortable in Kitty's dungeon. And then earlier today as she'd sat on top of him she'd seemed right at home. But right now she was blushing furiously and her fists were curled into tight little balls.

'What do you mean? I like it fine. As much as any other.'

'No, you don't. This makes you uncomfortable. Why? You weren't one of those naughty schoolgirls who had an affair with her teacher, were you?'

When her face fell Cash's heart fell with it. She'd got it on with a teacher? He'd assumed Faith was sexually adventurous but hadn't considered that she'd been so outrageous as a teenager. But maybe that was why she was so interested in all this. Maybe she'd had some older man show her the ropes when she was young. For some reason the idea of some dirty old man leering at her teenage arse made a ripple run through him.

'Faith. I'm sorry. I was only joking. I didn't actually think...'

'It wasn't like that.' He looked closer. Hers wasn't the face of a sexually satisfied teenager. It was something closer to sadness and a little bit of fear. His blood started pumping.

'What was it like, then?' He tried to remember where

she'd said she'd gone to school. Somewhere in England. He'd be in London next month; he wondered how long it would take to track this dirty old man down.

Faith looked small and very young in her school uniform. She brought her knees up to her chin.

'I was naïve and stupid and did something I shouldn't have.'

'What?' He gritted his teeth.

'He was my teacher. It only happened a couple of times.'

'Did he…did he make you do something you didn't want to?' Cash's jaw clamped shut.

'It wasn't like that. I…I chased him.'

'How old were you?'

'Seventeen. Old enough to know better.'

'Young enough to be fooled by an older man.'

'I wasn't fooled, I was in…'

'What…love? You were in love with him?' Something sparked in Cash's head. She still felt the sting of having her heart broken. That sting had turned into more of a burning numbness for him. Although his mind had wandered back to Jess more often since he'd been back in Australia, he realised he wasn't angry about it any more. He looked at the sadness on Faith's face. That was what he felt too. Sad that it had changed the way he thought about love and sex and trust.

'I thought I was. He paid attention to me. Told me things I wanted to hear,' she said, her voice soft and her accent broadening.

'That's not love. Love is when two people care about each other—not just when one person has the complete power over another.' Like Jess had over him right from the beginning. She'd known how he felt about her. She'd known he was besotted and she had manipulated him to get what she wanted. To get closer to Charlie.

Faith's eyes met his. There was a hint of glaze over them

as if a tear was close to the surface. 'I thought you didn't believe in love.'

Cash shrugged. 'I believe people think they're in love. But it's just a fairy tale. It always ends. I don't believe in happy ever afters and you shouldn't either.'

'Why?'

'Because when you love someone, you trust them. And when you trust someone you'll always be disappointed.'

'Not always.'

'Always. Who else have you loved, Faith—besides this joker who used you?'

'No one. Except my family. My parents, my brothers.'

'And have you ever felt betrayed by them?'

Faith hesitated. 'I felt betrayed when my parents sent me away to school. And my brothers teased me constantly about what happened. They still do.'

'The people who love us have the power to hurt us the most. That's why I try not to love anyone.'

'That's why sex is just sex for you.'

'Exactly. Simple. Uncomplicated.'

'Unable to get hurt.'

She made it sound as if he was scared. 'Why put yourself into a situation where you're sure to get hurt? The smart thing to do would be to avoid that altogether.'

'The smart thing, or the easy thing? Love exists so you can feel it. Don't you remember what it feels like to be in love? Isn't it wonderful?'

It was. For twelve months. Then it felt as if his heart were being ripped out through his nostrils. 'It's not worth the pain.'

'So you'd rather go through life feeling nothing so you don't have to experience the pain?'

'I don't feel "nothing". I have friends and I like my job. I'm content.'

'Content? Content is a word used by people who are too afraid to risk it all. Being content is not the same as the feeling of being in love. Love feels like you're flying and sick all at once. I want to feel that. I want to think about someone all the time and feel invincible.' Faith had let go of her knees and was looking more like herself again. Optimistic. Animated. Faithful. Gorgeous. 'Like my heart is so swollen it'll burst through my chest. Like nothing anyone can say or do can hurt me.'

'But you do get hurt. This teacher…this…predator. He hurt you. I'd suspect pretty bad by the way you can't get through this scene. Was the love worth all this pain?' As the words left his mouth he knew he shouldn't have said them. His honesty always got him into trouble. Like when he told Jess that Charlie had the hots for her. Like when he told Charlie that Jess seemed to be pulling away from him.

Faith looked up at him then and seemed to consider her answer. She looked away, out to the ocean, and finally after more than a minute of silence she spoke. 'No. It wasn't.'

He should have felt relief or some kind of triumph. He'd won the argument. He'd convinced her love wasn't worth it. But he didn't feel good. As he watched all the hope vanish from her heart, he once again felt like the world's biggest jerk.

Taking a breath, Cash moved closer to the bed. She didn't move so he sat on the edge and rested his hands on his knees. Love. This was why he didn't believe in it. Someone always got their heart broken.

'What about you? Who was she?'

Cash turned back to Faith, who had now extended her legs out so her toes were next to him. Her skin, so close he could touch it if he wanted to. His eyes trailed up her body, past that short school dress and on to her face. He knew what she was asking.

'She was a girl who worked on our farm as a roustabout. From the day I met her I couldn't think of anything else, anyone else. She was gorgeous and fun and could keep up with the men in the shed. She'd take their insults and give them right back. She was fearless and exciting and I'd never met anyone like her.'

'Did you love her?'

CHAPTER FOURTEEN

SOMETHING ABOUT THE way Faith asked made him keep eye contact. She wanted to know and he wanted to tell her. To tell her that she wasn't alone.

'I did at the time. As much as a twenty-year-old boy can love someone. We got together fast, it heated up fast. She seemed to like me as much as I liked her. But then...' Cash paused. He hadn't thought about Jess in a long time. It was easier in the States but being back home in Australia was bringing it all back. The heartbreak, the betrayal, the fight.

Faith cocked her head on one side, listening. Interested.

'But then my brother came home from uni and she chose him.'

'She left you for your brother? Cash, I'm sorry.'

Cash turned away; he didn't want her pity.

'It was inevitable. My brother Charlie was the one everyone wanted to be around. He was bigger than me, stronger than me, faster than me. Making people love him came easily to Charlie. He was friendly and easy and open. I was quieter, I kept to myself.'

'It still hurts when they choose someone else.'

He knew that. Especially since it was the man he'd been competing with his whole life. The one person he could never beat at anything.

Cash shrugged. 'You can't force someone to love you. She left me for him, and they're still together. Madly in love.'

'Oh, Cash.' Cash felt her hands on his shoulders. He should have pushed her away but he didn't. It felt good to have her there. It felt good to talk to someone who knew what it felt like.

'Were you and your brother close before that?'

'Very close. We're twins.'

'You're twins? Cash, that must have been awful.' Her hands curled even closer around his shoulders. Her fingers were small and her palms warm. His shoulders slumped a little, enjoying the way she was starting to rub her thumbs into his muscles. She'd shifted her legs up to get closer to him. Her breath teased the back of his ear, making the hair on the back of his neck stand on end. He held his hands steady; he didn't want to touch her. Didn't want to think about their kiss, but it kept coming back to him. The softness of her lips, the way the pad of her thumb caught the side of his lips and how her flesh tasted when he licked it.

'Did you argue?'

What? Right, Jess and Charlie.

'Yes. We fought. In the pub in the middle of town. Then out on the street.'

Faith's fingers continued to curl around him, pressing and rubbing. She moved even closer until he could feel her breasts up against his back. He leaned back a little, enjoying their softness and closing his eyes, thinking about that glimpse of hot pink he saw earlier.

'Then what happened?'

'Ah...' For a second he couldn't remember. 'The town started taking sides. People started to argue, my father got involved. We started to fight all the time. I had to leave.'

Faith's mouth was now near his ear. He'd only have to turn to feel her lips on his. 'That's awful, Cash. Are you and your brother over it now? Is everything all right?'

'No, we haven't spoken since.' He wanted to kiss her. He wanted to touch her and see her and he didn't give a damn that she was his employee. He wanted her. But when he turned, her hands flew off his shoulders and her eyes were open wide, staring at him.

'You haven't spoken since? How long ago was this?'

Cash frowned. What were they talking about again? Right. Charlie. Still interfering in his love life. 'Nine years.'

She reeled back to sit on her ankles, her hands now squarely on her hips. 'You haven't spoken to your twin brother in nine years? All because of some girl who didn't appreciate you?'

'He betrayed me.'

'*She* betrayed you. He did the wrong thing. But he is your brother. Your twin brother. You don't give up on relationships like that.'

Cash moved back. His brother stole the woman he loved. That was unforgivable. An unwritten brotherly rule.

'I didn't do anything wrong here, he did.'

'All he did was fall in love with someone he shouldn't have. We've all done that. You let her come between you. That must have been some great sex you two had!'

Sex with Jess was good. But it was twenty-year-old's sex. He'd had much better sex since then. 'It wasn't about the sex.'

'What was it, then? You talk about sex being all about power. It seems like this woman still has power over you— she's still controlling you and you two are not even having sex any more.'

Jess had controlled him. But he'd learned never to let anyone control him since. He'd worked his way to the top of the TV game by being in charge all the time, by wielding the power, not being in anyone else's power.

'Jess doesn't control me.'

'She controls your relationship with your brother. All because you two once had sex.'

'We didn't just have sex. It was more than that.'

'What was it?'

'We were…' In love? He'd thought they were at the time, but now? She'd loved that he looked like Charlie. He'd found out later she'd got the job on his father's farm just to meet Charlie—she'd had a crush on him for years. That he got to her first was just a distraction to her until her true conquest arrived. He'd loved the attention she gave him. He'd loved the way he felt when he was with her. Strong, powerful, someone worth getting to know. For the first time he hadn't been in Charlie's shadow. She had been his and he was somebody. He was Cash—not just Charlie's twin.

'What were you?' Faith prompted, bringing him back to her.

'Stupid. Naïve. I thought because we were having sex we were automatically in love. But we weren't. Like I said—sex is just sex.'

'Except it wasn't for you. It was so much more. Sex is never just sex.'

Cash paused. His chest filled and deflated. Sex with Jess had been all about him feeling like someone special—someone unique. It had made him feel as if he'd finally won. Sex with Faith wouldn't be about sex either. It would be the answer to how he felt right now. Frustrated, angry, powerless. He wanted to win. He wanted to have her.

'You're right, Faith. Sex isn't just sex. It always means more, and that's the problem. This teacher who gave you attention—sex for him was about living out some sick fantasy. Jess had sex with me because I looked like someone else. And neither of those reasons sound like very good reasons to have sex.'

Faith's eyes were hard. He knew she was angry. He knew what she thought of him—someone who let a girl get between him and his brother. Someone with too much pride and not enough sense. Then she did something that surprised him. She shuffled her knees and moved closer until her breasts were right under his chin. They were straining against the school uniform and he longed to dip his head and kiss them through the thin fabric. But he didn't because her blue eyes were on his and when she looked at him like that he couldn't turn away. Carefully she placed a hand on his jaw. He hadn't shaved that morning and she rubbed the bristles there.

'They're not good reasons to have sex. Two people should have sex because they care about each other and because they want to show that other person how they feel.'

She came even closer and Cash's jeans strained hard against his skin. He wanted to move to make himself more comfortable but he didn't dare. One centimetre and his mouth would be on her breast.

She moved her finger and traced his mouth with it. His lips tingled under her touch. A heat started to burn in him, a wall of fire that seemed to be burning out of control inside his skin. He reached for her, stroking her jaw the way she did to him. Her skin was satin soft. He let his thumb trace her jawline and heard her gasp a little when he hit her lip.

'Or they could just have sex because they're hot for each other,' he murmured—trying to keep this thing under his control. Trying with everything he had to keep thinking instead of just feeling the way he wanted to. Trying to convince himself he had this under control.

Her breathing got heavier, her chest lifted up and down and he couldn't resist any longer. He let his mouth touch her breast and used his teeth to bite down so she could feel him there. A gentle nip that would tell her exactly what he wanted to do.

Faith's surprised gasp spurred him on. He kissed her shoulder through the fabric of the dress and let his hands fall to her thigh. Slowly and carefully he trailed his fingers up her leg. She didn't move. His eyes met hers and her lips parted. She looked so beautiful kneeling before him. Her eyes trusted him; he wanted to hold her—to take care of her—to reassure her that not all men would treat her badly. Maybe it was time he let go. Maybe he should let someone in. Maybe he could trust her. Slowly he leaned in and touched his lips to hers. It was as if a long drink of water was being poured down his throat after being in the dusty desert for days. Sweet relief.

He lifted his hand higher until he felt the lace of her underwear. Hot pink. Slowly, his eyes not leaving hers, he let his fingers slip in between the lace and her skin. He dipped his fingers and felt her. Waiting for him. Hot and wet and ready. A surge of something hard and powerful reared through him. He needed to kiss her; he had to taste her lips and feel her shiver beneath him. When his mouth met hers, it wasn't gentle this time. It was hard and desperate and it made her fall backwards onto the bed but he caught her before she fell against it—making sure she didn't hurt herself as her head hit his pillow.

'Cash, I thought you said you didn't like me.' Her voice was a little shaky, as if she was nervous.

He didn't remember saying he didn't like her. Of course he liked her.

'I want to have sex with you, Faith. I want to get you off and make you scream my name.'

'But do you care about me?'

Something about the way she asked made him stop. She was frightened. Vulnerable. What if he hurt her?

He kissed her again, with everything he was feeling, to try and make her understand. It was a hot, hard, needy kiss that had him feeling a little out of control.

'Cash?' she breathed when he pulled away.

'I don't know,' he whispered against the side of her face.

She sucked in a deep breath and when he tried to kiss her again, she turned her head.

Damn. Too honest.

'Faith, stop worrying. Think of it as research. Maybe your next show could be about orgasms and how to have the most powerful one of your life, which—I assure you—I won't stop till you have.' A deep wrinkle formed between her eyes. She gripped his biceps hard and pushed. He pulled back.

'I thought you said this show was my last.' She struggled to sit up and, reluctantly, he let her. He didn't want to. He wanted her to shut up. He wanted to throw her back on the bed and kiss her entire body but he knew that wasn't going to happen. Not now. Not when she realised who he really was. An inconsiderate bastard who spoke before he thought. Someone who didn't deserve to be loved by anyone. 'Are you telling me that if I have sex with you you'll keep my show on?'

It was his turn to be confused. He hadn't said that. 'No.'

'Yes.' She sat up completely now and pushed him right off. 'That's exactly what you're saying. A couple of hours ago you were reminding me that this was my last show, but now, just as we're about to have sex, you propose I do another show.'

'It was a joke, Faith.'

'A joke? A joke to try and get me to sleep with you?' She stood up, her face red and her temper well and truly up. 'I don't think you're very funny. How could I be so stupid… again? To think that a kiss meant something it didn't. To think you could actually care about me when you don't even believe in love.' She jumped off the bed and started pulling on the zipper at the back of her dress. 'It's this dress, isn't it? It's turning you on, isn't it? That girl Jess treated you as if you didn't matter. She hurt you worse than anyone ever could, and yet you learned nothing. You still think sex is just sex and that it's OK to treat me as if I don't matter. To you I'm just another girl who doesn't matter.'

Faith pulled at the dress, but it was futile; the zipper was stuck. She was angry and hurt and humiliated. Mr Turner had told her he'd make sure she had an A on the next exam. That had hurt her more than anything. As if she'd slept with him to get good marks. She'd slept with him because she'd cared for him, and she was mortified that she'd almost made the same mistake with Cash.

'You're blowing this all out of proportion. I tell the truth,

Faith. I'm honest. Whether you like it or not—honesty is always better than lying.'

'There's honest, and then there's what you do. Say everything out loud that pops into your ignorant head.'

'I'm sorry. I told you before—I don't believe in love and I know that's what you want.'

Faith stopped. He was right: love was what she wanted. Was that so bad? Faith stopped tugging on the zipper. 'I can do the next two fantasies on my own. Voyeurism and exhibitionism. I don't need you for those. Just make sure you come to the burlesque club tonight. And, Cash…' She turned and let her eyes catch his hard. The flash of green in his left eye stood out. She'd been so close to his eyes a moment ago. She'd felt herself falling moments ago. Watching him as he watched her, sure he finally felt what she did. 'You win. I don't believe in love any more either.'

CHAPTER FIFTEEN

THE IRONIC HIPSTERS in the room started to twitter and take their seats. The women adjusted their black-rimmed glasses and the men brushed the crumbs from their beards. The show was starting. Cash twisted his neck from side to side and resisted the urge to slip a finger in between his collar and his skin. It was hot and the achingly cool crowd around him were starting to make him itch. He'd debated whether to come at all. Faith wouldn't want to see him after what happened this afternoon, but he'd promised her he'd help her and, whether she admitted it or not, she needed him. As her cameraman, and as her friend. He had to talk to her. He had to explain.

A blonde in a low-slung pair of jeans peered up at him through her eyelashes. This wasn't his scene. All this obvious sizing one another up. All the discreet looks from underneath fake eyelashes. It felt contrived, planned and manipulative. Perhaps it was his cynical nature but the place screamed sham. This bar with its faux 1920s décor and its cheap chandeliers and sugar-laced drinks was nothing but a trussed-up strip club. A place where desperate men paid to watch desperate women take their clothes off. All lies.

He spotted Faith near the back, talking to a redhead wearing sunglasses and a short skirt. He watched as Faith settled into her seat. He watched the way she smiled and laughed and flicked her ponytail off her shoulder. He'd been thinking of her all afternoon. He missed her. Her laughing and her teasing and her moments of utter vulnerability. He missed all of it and he still didn't know why. He wasn't supposed to want her. He wasn't supposed to like her, so why did her outburst this afternoon keep going through his mind? Over and over. *'To you I'm just another girl who doesn't matter.'* He hadn't just heard her pain when she'd said that—he'd felt it. He'd treated her exactly like the dirty old teacher of her youth. He'd used her, the way Jess had used him, and it made him feel sick to his stomach.

Cash moved to the side of the room and set up the cameras. One was to be focused on the stage and the other on Faith—they could edit out everything they didn't want later. He peered through the lens and watched her laugh. He zoomed in to her face, her smile, and his chest constricted. She had a beautiful smile. A smile that made him forget and eyes that made him focus. He stepped back. Away from the lens and away from the ridiculous thoughts coursing through his head.

The slow wailing of a trumpet pierced through the air and the moustached host in his ironic bow tie and checked suit pranced onto the stage. He started with a pathetic comedy routine before introducing the upcoming burlesque dance as performance art. He outlined in excruciating detail the political satire that was about to unfold and Cash watched in bemused fascination as the audience lapped up every word of his patronising lecture.

Cash wondered if Faith really believed all this. Did she actually think this was art, or did she know it for what it was? An act.

Faith leaned over to whisper to the woman wearing sunglasses, then turned her head and looked around before catching his eye. Her expression went still before she flashed a hesitant smile and his gut lurched. Her white teeth glowed against her red lips and she beckoned to him to join her. He felt the familiar pull of desire for her. A desire he was finding it hard to quell. But he had to. Faith made him do things he would never do. Feel things he shouldn't feel. She provoked him and distracted him and he was too busy to be distracted. And he was her boss. But he was finding it unusually hard to get her out of his mind and that was what was bugging him the most.

He glanced at her friend in those ridiculous sunglasses— now, she was more like it. Skirt too short, smile too wide, laugh too loud. Friendly. Easy. Uncomplicated. Trouble was, he felt absolutely no change in his physical condition when he looked at her, but his chemicals spun out of control every time Faith raised an eyebrow at him.

Leaving the cameras to do their work, he wound his way around the crowd and found himself standing next to Faith. She shifted so he could sit next to her. She didn't say anything; he guessed she was still angry about this afternoon. He didn't blame her. She was right. He did have a tendency to say everything that was on his mind—even if it meant someone was sure to get hurt.

A dinging bell made the host jump and finally shut up. Faith moved closer to Cash and he stopped himself just in time from slinging his arm around her shoulder and snuggling her in close. She had a way of looking at him with a playful expression on her face and making him think she was his, that they were there together. This was work. He was only here because he'd promised her he would see this through. He'd promised her a chance to prove herself. As he'd stolen her faith in love, he owed it to her to be there.

'You made it,' she whispered. She didn't sound angry and that made him feel even worse. She was understanding and sweet and didn't deserve to be treated the way he'd treated her. As if she didn't matter. Because she did. He snuck another look at her, letting his eyes fall down her nose and onto her full lips. She definitely mattered.

'I never miss the opportunity to see a woman strip.'

'It's not a strip club, it's burlesque. They don't take everything off and there won't be any ping-pong balls here.'

He laughed at her expression and relaxed a little. He liked being with Faith. She was a little guarded but he liked the way she always stood up to him. Instead of making him angry, it made him feel as if she was listening. As if *he* mattered.

Something about that thought stung at him. He wondered if Jess had ever actually made him feel that way. She'd held his hand and looked into his eyes and made him feel important, but he hadn't taken too much notice of what she said and what she did. It had been all about him and how it made him feel. About beating Charlie.

Being with Faith was different. He wasn't competing with anyone. He didn't need to win and she kept reaching for him and soothing him and he wondered why. Why didn't she just give up and walk away? Why was she still here, talking to him, making him feel special? He certainly didn't deserve it. He couldn't think about Faith as someone he could matter to. That was dangerous. Trusting someone was dangerous and she shouldn't trust him either.

The slit in her skirt fell away to reveal a nice portion of golden thigh and Cash's mind buzzed. Pure lust, he told himself. A physical reaction to a beautiful woman, that was all this was. He shifted, moving away from her, but she shifted too and he found her thigh millimetres from his again and he realised he wanted her there. Not just because she was gorgeous, but because he wanted to know how she was. He wanted her to know that he thought she mattered.

CHAPTER SIXTEEN

'LADIES, GENTLEMEN AND all you cats in between, the time has come to introduce you to the lovely, the gorgeous—the most mind-blowing woman alive—Miss Betty Boom-Boom!'

The crowd let up a wild cheer as the bongos started a regular beat. Faith smiled up at Cash and he looked away—at the stage, at the back of the head of the woman in front of him, anywhere but into Faith's bright, trusting eyes.

The band chimed in with lots of trumpet, plenty of hip-shaking bass and a truckload of kitsch. A leg appeared and then the tall, curvy body of the dancer appeared and wolf whistles went up from all across the room to show their appreciation.

Cash shifted again. Faith was moving, wiggling and straining her neck to get a better view and her bare calf met with his leg. When he glanced at her he could see the pulse beating in the hollow of her throat. Her skin glowed and he wanted to touch her. To press his lips right to that spot. To make that smile disappear and a moan escape from her lips. Everything inside him prickled with heat. His whole body was tense. He needed to calm down. He had to stop noticing every little thing about her. He had to prove to himself he was still in charge, which was why he did what he did next.

Leaning in close enough for his breath to touch her ear, he lowered his voice until it resembled gravel and murmured suggestively, 'Are you excited yet?'

The atmosphere between them changed in an instant. The smile disappeared from her lips and she went still. Even the way she was sitting seemed to change. She curled her spine up until she was sitting stiff and still, lifting her chin so he could see the long column of her neck. His plan had back-fired. Now, rather than being in control, he felt it slipping.

He was aware of her in a way he'd never been before. He wanted to be next to her. He wanted to touch her and hold her and keep her close and he knew that she wanted to touch him. He couldn't miss it. The way her breathing changed, the way her cheeks went pink, the way she deliberately kept her eyes forward. She'd felt the hot hit of connection between them but he wasn't sure what she was going to do with that information. Would she walk out? She should. That was ex-actly what she should do.

His words had been meant to disarm her—make her ner-vous so he could gain some control—but now everything seemed to be spiralling dangerously. His eyes travelled down to her chest and his eyes snagged on the perfect curve of her breasts. They curved and tipped up, her nipples were stand-ing erect and she wore a bra that pushed them up over the top of her dress. His eyes continued their journey, past the slight curve of her belly and over her hips to her legs. His collar rubbed against his skin. She shifted and leaned in closer—her eyes not leaving the stage. Probably to tell him off again. Good. He deserved it. He tried to turn his head to the stage and not look at her but he couldn't. He was only interested in watching her.

'Watch,' she whispered, her voice low and husky and shooting heat straight to his groin. 'Watch the way she moves, the way her eyes and hands tell you what she wants you to do. She leads you to where she wants you to look.'

He dragged his eyes off her full red lips and onto the stage. The woman was dressed in a long, tight dress cov-ered in sequins. Her hips moved when she walked and her gloved fingers ran trails over her body. As he watched his pulse thumped in his wrists. Faith's thigh was so close to his. He wanted to shift his leg to feel her against him. He wanted to lift his hands and place them on her skin, relieving the thumping ache that was now spreading through his body. She'd want more and he couldn't give her more. He knew that but right now he didn't give a damn. He just wanted her.

'She wants you to pay attention to how feminine she is. See the way she walks across the stage? Moving her hips so you look. Then she runs her hands up her body, over her breasts.' Breathing got harder as he listened to Faith's voice. Every pulse point he had was pumping blood faster than it ever had before. Her words skated over his skin like a cold breeze. Everything was standing to attention. Cash shifted his legs wider apart to make more room. His leg finally touched her thigh and he sucked in a breath; it felt as good as he'd imagined. Electric.

Sparking with someone was rare. Normally he saw their face, their body, their breasts. He wanted them physically. But this was different. There was a caution in the air between them. Something forbidden. Something he couldn't resist. He flicked his eyes to her, to see if she noticed it too, and she was looking at him. Right at him. Deep into him. He didn't want her to look at him like that but in that second it was exactly what he wanted. Her small pink tongue darted out to sweep across her bottom lip.

'Then she touches her face, her lips. She wants you to look. She wants you to notice. That's why this is the number one fantasy. Stripping for your man means he is only thinking about one thing. You.'

Faith drew her bottom lip in between her teeth and sucked. Cash couldn't move. His hands itched to touch; his body burned with the desire to be on top of her. Despite the knowledge that she was going to hate him when this all went pear-shaped. The way she let her lip bounce back out and the way her eyes moved ever so slowly to his lips made him forget everything except her. And his own body, which was now raging out of control.

'All women want to feel desired and valued and respected.' Cash looked into her eyes. Her lashes were dark and the navy irises were now almost black. He clenched his gut, holding on, waiting. Faith moved closer, her breath leaving heat marks on his chin. She was going to kiss him. And he wasn't going to stop her. Even though somewhere in his brain he knew he should.

'Sex is never just sex for a woman. Sex is about how you make her feel.'

Faith moved back, suddenly. 'And if you make her feel used, you better watch out because there's nothing more painful than dealing with a woman who's been hurt.' Cash's mouth dried up completely. He hadn't wanted to hurt her; he hadn't wanted it to go this far. He hadn't wanted to feel anything for her—but she was the type of person you couldn't ignore. Faith turned back to the stage, leaving Cash with his mouth open, unsure of what to say to her. He wanted to apologise; he wanted to reassure her that he never meant to hurt her, but anything he said would have just been words and she deserved more than that.

'See how she teases? She's taunting the men. Showing them what they'll never have.'

Her sensual mouth moved into a wicked smile. The dimple in her cheek was back. She looked playful and fun and sexier than he'd ever seen her look.

'They tease and taunt and make him think he's won.' She smiled up at him, looking far more beautiful than she ever had. 'Then they take it away. They move on to the next man. She has the power and all the men are just her toys.'

Cash's heart stopped in his chest. This wasn't about her and him at all; it was about teaching him that sex wasn't just sex. She'd said she didn't believe in love any more and this was her telling him what she did believe in. Power. And she had it. Just as Jess had it. Over him. Heat crept up into his brain. He was being played again. He'd let his weak country-boy heart think that there was something between them and now she was teaching him that that was a stupid thing to do.

Faith had learned about more than tassels and feathers from the women here at the burlesque club. She'd learnt the female art of manipulation. She knew how to draw people in. To let them think she wanted more. Only to pull away at the last minute. She was a tease. And he was too smart to fall for that trick again. For a moment he'd lost control. He'd let himself think too far ahead and he knew that was wrong. Trust no one. He'd been living by that motto for the past nine years.

'Isn't it just like a woman to make an art form out of deception? To promise something she has no intention of delivering.'

The smile froze on her face but it left her eyes. 'She's not promising anything.'

'She's promising everything.' The fire that was running through his veins had now turned liquid hot. He wanted her to feel the way he did. Disappointed. Angry. Let down. 'But it's all lies. Lies and deception. Which is all your show is.'

Faith blinked and the smile faded from her lips. He hated that he'd done that to her. He hated that a minute ago she seemed hot for him and now she'd gone cold. But he was angry. Jess had tricked him. She'd made him believe they were in love and now Faith was doing the same thing, to get what she wanted.

He moved his leg so it was no longer touching hers. He didn't want to be near her. He wanted to be at the bar buying a drink for a leggy blonde. Someone who didn't rattle him. Someone he felt nothing for. Someone who didn't make him say things he shouldn't and think things he couldn't.

Faith's eyes left his and she turned back to the stage. She rested her hands on either side of her thighs and her spine went all stiff again. She shrugged one shoulder slowly. 'It's different for women, Cash. Our power is not physical, it's

mental. It's our ability to out-think and outsmart. To stay
two steps ahead. It's what we do to protect ourselves. From
people who want to hurt us.' Her eyes flicked to him. 'Those
women on stage are aware of their power. Up there, she can
make a man do whatever she wants. She can make him fall
in love. She can make him want her like he's never wanted
anything in his life. She can control him. That's the power
of burlesque.'

Cash shifted but didn't take his eyes off her. Something
was happening. Her eyes were challenging him.

'These men don't really want her. They're being manipulated. It's not real and neither is her power. All of this is a
lie. An illusion. Just an act.'

'Maybe. But aren't we all acting? Pretending to know
more than we do. Pretending not to feel what we feel. Even
you, I suspect.' Those eyes of hers held him steady. 'You
talk of honesty like you don't tell lies. You want everyone
to think you're the most honest man in the room, but you're
hiding like the rest of us. The difference is you're too scared
to admit it.'

She had no idea what she was talking about. Scared?
Him? When he was a cameraman, he'd come face to face
with terrorists and been in the middle of war zones. Nothing scared him. Except her. Right now, the way she was
looking at him made his heart scud across his chest as if
it'd been crash tackled by the entire back line of the Welsh
rugby team.

'You want to know the truth?' Her eyes flicked back to
his and she considered him. He waited until he had her full
attention; he waited until he saw her eyes move to his lips
and watch as his words formed. 'I want you, Faith. In my
bed. Right now. I want to have sex—just sex. With you.'

CHAPTER SEVENTEEN

FAITH SWALLOWED HARD as she watched Cash's lips move. She saw the words form on his lips but the catcalling and yelling from the crowd made it hard for her to hear. What she thought she heard was that he wanted her. In his bed. Right now.

She couldn't look into his eyes. She'd wanted to hurt him. She'd wanted him to feel a little of the way she'd felt this afternoon. Used and unwanted. But for some reason nothing ever went simply with Cash. He caught her out every time. As if by just looking into her eyes he could see the truth. But she didn't want him to know the truth. She didn't want just sex with him. She wanted more. When he looked at her like that, as if he was really seeing her, she could feel her body melting.

He'd said this afternoon that he was there for her. He'd told her that he was there for her if she needed him and she'd even started to believe him. Especially when he'd opened up about his past. But then he'd said she could have another show and everything had spiraled. She couldn't even remember what she'd said to him. She wasn't even sure any more what she felt—all she knew was that it was all getting confused. Sex, love—she had no idea what it was all about and she wondered if she ever would.

Faith turned away, her brain ticking and her body buzzing. The heat of him so close warmed her bare skin. Her skin ached to feel his. She didn't want to feel this. She wanted to like him less. She wanted it to just be about sex but every time his eyes snagged on hers she felt more. But she didn't want to feel more. Not with him. Not with someone she was sure wouldn't be able to return her feelings. She just wanted to push what she felt down deep where she'd pushed everything else.

Cash didn't touch her but she could feel him next to her, his body pulsing with heat and anticipation. His arm brushed hers as he reached for the drink in front of her and he met her eyes with that intense stare. He wanted to drink her drink. She nodded and he picked it up and took a sip. His lips touched the glass right where hers had been moments ago. Something inside her froze. Somehow that small action of him drinking her drink seemed even more intimate than the kisses they'd shared or the way he'd touched her on his bed. He was sharing her drink. Trusting her. Letting her know that they were together. But they weren't, and she needed to stop thinking about him as someone who could care about her. She knew what he wanted and that was all he'd ever want.

She tried to think but here in this club, filled with slow sensual music and hot bodies beating with anticipation, it was hard to think. She knew if she took him up on his offer it would just be sex. But sex was never just sex. Not for her.

'Faith?' His deep voice growled in her ear and she jumped. 'Did you hear what I said?'

She didn't look at him but kept her eyes on the stage, her chin up. 'I heard you.'

'Then what do you say?'

Faith raised her eyes and met his dark stare. Perhaps she should see this through. Perhaps this was exactly what she needed to do. Maybe she could use him the way other men used her. Maybe she'd finally learn what it felt like to have an orgasm with someone other than herself. A shiver ripped through her.

She didn't love him and he couldn't ever love her; this would just be physical. And she'd be safe as long as it stayed that way. She was safe as long as… The touch of his thumb tracing her cheek stopped every thought in her head. He had moved in closer. She turned to him and his eyes roamed her face before settling back on hers and locking. Hard. His eyes were so beautiful. So dark they seemed to go on for ever. She could drown in them.

A sleepy fog spread throughout her body. The way he looked at her was making it hard for her to think straight. But she had to. She had to figure out what to do. She had to figure out if seeing through this chemistry they shared would lead to closure—or would it just slash open a wound she'd taken care to keep very securely stitched up?

'Perhaps you should find someone else, someone who shares your philosphy on life and love.' His eyes slid to her lips as she spoke and it became harder not to push closer but she didn't. She stayed still until his eyes returned to hers.

'I don't want anyone else. I want you.' Faith's cheeks burned and she had to turn away. *I want you.* No one had ever said that to her. Definitely not with the intensity with which he'd just said it. *Let's do it. Why not?* She'd heard that. But never *I want you.* A simple sentence that made her heart ache. He didn't want her. It was a line. She knew that. She was feeling things she shouldn't feel again. She moved away from him.

'What you need is a night with a woman who can teach you what you're doing wrong.'

A crease formed between his eyes and Faith looked at it, transfixed.

'Maybe what you need,' he shot back, 'is to spend a night with someone who can teach *you* what you've been doing wrong.'

'I don't do anything wrong. Sex with me will be the high-light of your life.' She smiled—trying to keep it light—trying to establish that all-important barrier. But then he reached for her hand and held it. He didn't stroke or play with her. He just held her hand and let his other arm fall around her shoulders while his eyes held hers.

'I don't want to see your tricks. I want to see you.'

Something ached behind her breastbone. She couldn't breathe. Her stomach tumbled. She shifted so his arm fell off her shoulder but his hand held tight to hers.

Forcing a smile onto her face, she ground out, 'Don't be so quick to fob off my tricks—you haven't seen them yet.'

She was bluffing. She had no tricks. She had no idea what to do—she'd never had good sex. A few fumbles in the dark, that was all. But she couldn't let him know that.

His big arm encircled her shoulder again and he pulled her in with a strong, easy movement. So strong. So easy to trust, but she had to stay alert. Remember who he was and what he believed in. Lust. Sex. Definitely not love. He leaned down to her ear and a shiver spread over her shoulders and tickled down the backs of her arms at the feel of his hot breath. 'I want you, Faith,' he murmured.

Faith breathed. In and out. She wanted him too. Every pore of her skin screamed as he pressed up against her—hot and hard and big. She wanted him but she had no idea what to do with him. She would disappoint him and herself and the familiar feeling of shame and inadequacy would come back.

'If we do this, I want to make one thing clear.'

'Yes?' His expression turned hungry. His tongue came out to run across his bottom lip and everything in Faith's body seized.

'I'm in charge. I lead. You follow.' She thought that would turn him off. He seemed the type of man to want to be in control. But to her horror, he didn't disagree.

'If that's what you want. But you might change your mind. Often the woman who wants to be in charge is the very woman who likes to be controlled.'

'I don't want to be controlled. I want you to listen. And do what I say.'

He moved closer and she stayed still. His lips hovered above her ear and then he dipped his head. His lips brushed the skin at her nape and she shivered, not daring to move her arms in case all her much-needed control fled.

'I'll do what you say.' His teeth bared down onto the soft flesh on her neck and he bit down gently.

She let her head fall back a little as his tongue shot out to soothe the place he'd just bitten. She ached to touch him but she didn't.

'You'd better.' Her voice came out in a whisper.

His mouth moved around to her earlobe and he bit her again. She forced the whimper on her lips back in. When his mouth finally made its way to her cheek she turned her head—without thinking. She wanted her lips near his and she wanted his lips on hers.

'But if you do change your mind and want me to take control, be warned…' His hot breath went into her mouth and she turned more—seeking the hotness of his mouth. Wanting it but hating that she wanted it all at once. 'I'll make you beg.'

Images of begging him poured into her mind and she struggled to stay in control. His lips were soft and achingly tender when they kissed the corner of her mouth. She wanted to slump into him. She wanted to turn her head and let him kiss her deep and hard and long. But instead she turned her head and looked back at the stage, her heart hurting inside her chest as it beat furiously and her fingernails sore where they dug into the lounge.

'I won't change my mind.'

Thankfully, Cash turned back to the stage and didn't look at her. She was relieved because she wasn't sure every thought in her ridiculous head wasn't showing on her face. She wished she could get up and walk out but she couldn't do that. The cameras were here and recording. She'd seen him set one up on her face. She'd go in and do the voice-overs tomorrow.

Right now, she wished there weren't any cameras on her.

And she didn't want to think about this show and the dancers and everything else she'd rave about in her report tomorrow. Right now all she wanted to do was feel Cash's warm arm slung behind her on the chair. Enjoy the way he smelled when he leaned in close. Experience the way her skin tingled when he spoke in her ear—his voice vibrating through her. What she wanted to do was wrap herself around him—take every stitch of clothing off and be on top of him so she could see him. Watch his muscles move as he lifted his arms, see his face when they…

She had to do this. Now. Quickly she stood and felt his eyes on her. 'Let's go.'

'Now?'

'Now.'

Faith made it all the way to the door before she stopped. Cash was still there, at her back, and she was sweating. Could she really do this? This was mad. She'd be the one left hurt if it backfired. She'd spent her life thinking sex was never just sex. What if it was? What if they did it and he left and that was it? Or what if it was her who didn't feel anything? Faith felt as if she were on the edge of something and jumping meant everything would change for ever. Was she ready for that? No, this was a ridiculous idea. She turned to face him, looking up at him as he was now so close.

'You don't want me, Cash. Let me find you someone else. Let me introduce you to Betty.' He looked confused for a second, then angry, then, with a hand hovering above the small of her back, his eyes searched her face. 'Are you all right, Faith?'

She shifted as if to go around him but he stopped her. He brought his hands up to the tops of her arms and pulled her closer. His big, strong chest was pushed against hers. She wanted to curl herself up against him, breathe him in and let him hold her.

But she didn't.

She couldn't because then he'd leave and her heart would break.

Instead she smiled.

She nodded, adding a bright smile to her face. 'Of course. Are you?' She tried to keep her voice light and bright.

'Yes.' He sounded so definate. So resolute. 'Are you sure you're all right?'

He knew. He always knew when she wasn't telling the truth. 'Yes.'

Cash moved his body slightly closer to her and dropped his hand to slip it around her waist. It felt incredibly intimate and she looked around to see if anyone noticed. But no one was looking. His big body next to her was comforting.

'We don't have to do anything you don't want to. It's probably not a good idea anyway. You work for me.'

She didn't want him to be considerate or careful or nice. She wanted him to tell her again that she didn't mean anything to him.

'Not any more. You're cancelling my show, remember?'

'I can find you something else. There's a spot on the breakfast program that needs filling.'

She shook her head. 'No. It's time for me to move on.' She smiled up at him. She didn't want to move on. She wanted to stay but she had to leave. She felt awful and sad and disappointed. His body shifted even closer until all she could feel was him and all she could smell was him and all she could think of was him. Close and wanting to be with her. Wanting to comfort her when she needed it. Sex. That's what he was offering. Not love, just a token of his affection and she wanted to take it. For once she wanted sex to just be sex.

Faith shifted her arm and slipped her hand deep into his pocket, letting her fingers brush against him, enjoying the feel of him hardening beneath her touch. She wanted to feel him close. Even though she knew she was leaving and wouldn't ever come back. Even though she knew what he felt was not a tenth of what she did. Never would be.

She removed her hand abruptly but he caught it and placed it into the crook of his arm.

'Then there's nothing stopping us.'

She blinked. They were going to do this. They were going to have 'just sex'.

'Cash…'

'It's just me, Faith. You and me,' he said gently, and it was enough. Enough for her desperate heart to think that this wouldn't matter. That she could handle it.

Carefully she lifted herself up and pressed her lips to his. He didn't react violently but kissed her back, just as gently. When she opened her eyes he was looking at her, directly at her. The green in his left eye had her transfixed.

'I think it's time we left,' she whispered, and he didn't hesitate, just took her hand and led her out of the door.

CHAPTER EIGHTEEN

THE FEELING OF Cash's hand in hers and the hit of cool air when they stepped outside made Faith giddy. And when he pulled her into the laneway next to the club she knew she wasn't going to turn back. He kissed her hard and pressed her into the wall. His hands found the bottom of her shirt and when they touched her skin underneath she moved closer to him.

'I like the way you kiss,' she murmured. She wanted to hold back and keep her distance but the way his lips kept moving to her neck, the bristles along his jaw scratching at her sensitised skin, was making her forget everything else.

'You're not so bad yourself.' She felt his smile as he kissed back up her neck and placed a large hand around her jaw.

'I want to kiss you everywhere.'

'Then you should do it.' His eyes met hers and the fire between them raged. She couldn't help but think he felt it now. He had to feel this.

Placing her hands on his chest, she pushed, stopping his mouth from falling onto her neck again.

'Wait, Cash, wait.' He stilled and their eyes connected. 'Do you like me? Do you care about me?' She knew this was about sex. She knew that was all this was but something inside her had to be reassured. She had to know she was important to him.

His eyes slid from hers to her mouth, then back up again.

She held her breath, dreading his answer. She knew what he was going to say and she knew how it was going to make her feel.

'I like you right now. I want you right now. That's all I can offer you.'

Faith wanted to kiss him, she wanted to accept what he was saying but everything was so confused in her mind. The memory of how much it hurt when a man walked out the door was too vivid—too real—and somehow if it was Cash walking out, she was sure it would feel even worse. Should she do this? Could she do this? She needed some space, some air, so she pushed his chest hard until no part of him had any contact with her body. Then she let her hands slide away and quickly, before she could change her mind, she walked away.

She hadn't expected this to happen; she hadn't expected to feel so much for him and she just couldn't decide if she could handle it when he walked out the door.

'Faith, stop running.'

His voice made her start to walk faster. She couldn't deal with him right now. She needed to be alone.

'Faith, stop.' His arm was on her elbow and he swung her around. His eyes were dark and his usually neat hair was sticking up everywhere where she'd run her fingers through it. He looked a little wild and very angry.

'Let me go.'

'No, not until you tell me what the hell is going on. Tell me what you want, Faith. Be honest. Tell me.'

'I have no idea, Cash. I don't know what I want. I thought I wanted this. I thought I wanted you but now…I can't do this.'

His touch was warm and it was helping her heart slow down. She was being irrational and emotional. Why was she getting so worked up? Why couldn't they just have sex without it meaning anything more? Cash was just someone she was attracted to. Someone who made her feel better. Someone she helped when he needed her. That was all this was.

Wrapping her arms around herself, Faith walked defiantly to the side of the bridge they were now on and stopped about a metre from the edge. If she saw the water, she'd panic—she'd always been afraid of heights and right now they were up far too high.

Boats bobbed along the docks and the noise of people laughing and talking rose up from the restaurants below. He moved silently past her to the rail and leaned back against it, looking at her, his hands tucked firmly in his pockets. Panic rose in Faith's throat. He was too close to the edge.

'Come back away from the rail.' He looked behind him into the water and back to Faith.

He reached for her. 'Come here.'

Faith shook her head, wrapping her arms tighter around herself.

'Don't be frightened. Trust me. It's safe. Come here. Stand with me.'

He looked strong and stable standing there. Relaxed and at ease and she wanted to be close to him. She wanted to feel the comfort of his big body. But what if the railing fell? What if she leaned over too far?

'Faith.' He stepped forward and pulled her hands away from her body. 'Come with me.'

She watched his eyes. They held on hers and he stepped backwards. She shuffled forwards, swaying a little at the sight of the rail coming closer.

'Trust me, Faith, I have you,' he murmured, pulling on her hands again. She shuffled again, not taking her eyes off his until he pulled her into his body. She wrapped her arms around his waist and pressed her cheek to his heart. It thumped in her ear.

'I've got you, Faith.' His voice rumbled through his chest and into her head. She felt safe and warm and she never wanted to let him go. 'Look at me.' He gripped her arms and forced her back. 'Look at me.' She looked at him. His eyes travelled over her face, across her hair and down her neck. The sear of his gaze made her shiver. All of a sudden the noise of the people died away and her heart stopped in her chest.

'You asked me if I cared about you, and the answer is yes, I do. Of course I do. You're smart and funny and interesting and I want you. But I just can't offer any more. I can't give you any more.'

She knew what he was saying; she knew what he was offering and resolution landed on her thick and fast.

'I want you, Cash. I want to be with you, even if it's just sex. I want you.' Cash's eyes dipped and trailed along her cheek. He slid his hand down her arm till he was holding her hand. Slowly and carefully he twisted her arm until her fingers touched the metal of the railing behind him. She gasped, looking up at him then back down at her fingers, which were now gripping the iron rail with white knuckles. She was doing it. She was right at the rail.

'Look down,' he said, his hand not leaving hers and his other arm wrapped firmly around her waist. She let her eyes trail over his shoulders, across his chest and down further, where his waist narrowed. Drawing in a steadying breath, she tried to pull herself together. It was just a bridge. It was safe. He had her. She could do this. She shut her eyes tightly and moved her head back to face the water, waiting till the pulse in her neck slowed.

Faith opened her eyes. The water was black and it lapped at the pylons. She gripped the rail with one hand and Cash with the other. Her stomach heaved.

'I've got you,' he murmured in her ear. 'I've got you and I'm not letting go.'

She slumped into him. 'I want to do this.'

'Faith.' She turned at the sound of his voice and his eyes locked with hers. Hard. Something changed between them. What was once sizzling and hot now became raw and desperate. She wanted to move away but fear gripped her, making her heart stand still. Anticipation of what he was going to say made her mouth dry.

He watched her for a second, then turned to fix his eyes on a spot far out in the black water. His face in profile was almost as handsome as it was straight on. Strong brows led down his long, straight nose to his set, square jaw. She took a deep breath, then wished she hadn't as his scent assaulted her nostrils. Deep and spicy and male. His jaw pulsed once, twice and again before being still. Despite his casual stance, she could tell he was as affected as she was. He felt whatever this was between them. He shifted and Faith saw the muscles in his back and shoulders as they moved. Desire shot through her, hard and hot. Her nipples hardened painfully and a pulse throbbed at her core, right where she'd felt him pressed up against her in Patricia's garden the other morning. She wanted to reach out and touch him. So she did.

Cash realised she was no longer holding the rail, she was just holding him. This wasn't supposed to happen. It was supposed to be just sex.

Caution fired through him as he remembered how he'd tried to stay away from her tonight. But he'd missed her. And he knew he'd hurt her and that hurt him. With a force that surprised him. He'd thought he could handle this. A quick fling. Something casual. But every move she made tonight was smooth and sensual, as if she was moving deliberately because she knew he was watching. Every time she looked around he imagined it was for him, as if she could smell him in the air. As if she knew exactly what he wanted and wanted to give it to him. She was like a hit of a highly lethal street drug; she had a way of making him feel invincible, as if he were the most important person in the room. And he'd enjoyed the feeling of her focus so much he'd forgotten that he didn't want it.

But she wanted more. He should have let her run as she

wanted to. But the thought of her upset and missing him
made him angry. At himself, at her and at everything that
had happened between them. He wanted to be with her. Tonight. Tomorrow night. And after that. Which was absolutely crazy.

'You're not holding on.'

Faith looked down at the rail, then at the water, before
meeting his stare.

'No. I'm not.' She was taking a risk; he could see it. He
had to be the strong one here; he had to make sure this didn't
become something he couldn't handle, but when he looked
at her he wasn't sure if he wasn't falling for her. But still he
didn't say anything; he didn't tell her to stop. It was as if
there were something between them, pulling them together,
and there was nothing he could do about it.

He dipped his head and when his lips met her mouth
he drank her in. The way her skin smelled, the way her
lips tasted and the sexy way she let her tongue run slowly
along his bottom lip. After just a moment's hesitation, she
moved into his arms and her body arched as his arms came
around her, pulling her into the hardness of him. When she
moaned, he lost it. That noise she made at the back of her
throat was enough to make his smile disappear and a glint
of something animal take over him. She was his. He needed
her and she needed him.

'Faith,' he murmured.

His body hummed with want and she opened her lips to
him, and he let his tongue taste her mouth again.

'Cash.' Her voice came out as a husky moan. He pulled
away.

'Faith,' he replied, his breathing heavy as if he'd just
emerged from being under water too long. 'How far is it to
the water taxi?' he asked, a gruff rawness lacing his words.
Nothing was going to stop him from having her.

CHAPTER NINETEEN

FAITH SMILED. HE wanted it bad.

'It's just down there.' He grabbed her hand and pulled. They hurried across the bridge as fast as they could but Cash kept stopping to scoop her up into his arms and kiss her thoroughly. She smiled and laughed as if she were sixteen and being kissed for the first time. When he looked at her, his eyes were focused. She was the only thing he was looking at, the only thing he was thinking of. It made her feel important and special and strangely calm. Every step they took made the fear she'd felt before start to vanish. Sex. That's all this was. Then it would be over. She could do this. She had to do this. To move on, to feel whole again. She had to be able to think of sex as just sex. With her hand wrapped around his big bicep they walked beneath the bridge to the water-taxi dock but it was deserted. Cash pulled out his phone and called the number on the poster at the dock. He frowned.

'They'll be an hour.'

'An hour?'

'Busy night apparently. Parties all over the harbour.'

'I suppose we'll just have to wait.'

Cash sat on the wooden bench, then pulled her down to sit on his lap. His hand found her chin and he rested his fingers there as he kissed her. Faith let her hands explore his powerful shoulders, pushing her fingers beneath his jacket to feel the corded muscles strung across them. He put an arm around her hip and pulled her closer and she let herself wonder for just a second what it would feel like to do this all the time. Whenever she wanted. But that wasn't what this was about. This was about letting go of her fear and just having sex. With a gorgeous man.

'You taste delicious,' he mumbled, a smile spreading across his lips.

Faith laughed and nipped at his lip with her teeth. 'You are getting too carried away. It'll be another hour until we're in the taxi, then another twenty minutes before we get to my place.'

Cash groaned and brought his lips down onto hers again. 'I don't know if I can wait that long.' He watched her lips hungrily then met her eyes. Faith's breasts swelled and her nipples prickled to hardness. His impatience turned her on. He wanted her. As much as she wanted him. But this was just sex, she reminded herself. Just. Sex.

His eyes were hooded and beneath were as dark as the sky. His full lips were parted and she lifted a hand to rub across the roughness of the stubble on his cheek. The way he looked at her, as if there were no one else. As if he were seeing right inside her and he couldn't let her go. He was devouring her face with his eyes and she felt like his. As if she belonged to him alone and he belonged to her. Her heavy heart pounded. A light, reckless sensation of falling ran through her head. This didn't feel like 'just' anything.

'Cash.'

Something changed when she said his name. Faith didn't know why or how, but the look in his eyes changed. Suddenly the teasing left and he became serious.

'Faith,' he murmured as his large hand came up to cradle her chin again, more gently this time. She lifted her hand and traced one finger across his eyebrow and down his cheek as if memorising every plane and angle of his face. Memorising the way he was looking at her and how he made her feel. As if she were the only person that existed. As if she mattered. He pushed his thumb over her lips. She kissed it, opened her mouth and flicked her tongue across the tip and closed her eyes. His answering moan and the feel of his rock-hard erection beneath her let her know that he was enjoying it. He was enjoying her. She shifted so she could feel him against her. She wiggled and pushed herself down onto him.

Cash groaned. 'I'm not made of stone, Faith.'

He let his hand slip from her face and down her body. Her skin burned as he caressed her with his palm, across her breasts, past her stomach and over her hips. Sex, she reminded herself. This was just sex. She gasped as he slid his hand down her thigh and slipped it through the slit of her dress. He started the long slide back up her leg, his eyes not leaving hers. He moved slowly, seductively up and over her knee. He stopped to lean over and kiss the hollow at the base of her knee and she trembled. The warmth of his tongue and the wet feel of it slid straight up her leg, burning a trail right to her core. He shifted away and watched his hand as he pushed it further up her inner thigh. Her skirt came up and they could both see what he was doing and where his hand was going.

He was paying attention to her as no one ever had, as if every part of her was beautiful. As if he wanted every inch of her body. She felt like stopping him, he couldn't possibly want her that much, but she didn't. This felt like sex. Hot and animal. Pure lust. She watched, mesmerised, as his hand, dark against the pale skin of her thigh, moved higher. When he reached the thin layer of lace he pushed his thumb across her and she had to bite her tongue to stop crying out. Faith had never felt more wanted. His eyes were glued to hers; they were black as the sky. Direct. Sincere.

'Do you like that?' His voice was low and gruff.

She nodded. She couldn't speak.

He slipped one finger inside the lace of her underwear and brushed it against her, pushing the flimsy material aside.

'What if someone comes?' She could barely speak at

the waves of pleasure his lone finger was sending through her body.

'No one's coming,' he said, then smiled. 'Not yet, anyway.'

She couldn't believe what she was doing. On a public dock in a crowded city. But there was no one around and he was looking at her with such longing that she couldn't wait. Couldn't stop. And that was what this was about. Letting go. Being someone different. So she moved her thighs a little further apart. He made a noise in the back of his throat, almost like a growl, and slipped another finger in underneath the lace.

She whimpered, then moaned, then cried out in pleasure as his fingers slid along the slickness of her folds. His mouth pressed to hers and she kissed him desperately as his fingers pushed deep inside her. She wanted him to know how much she was enjoying this—how grateful she was that he was paying attention. That he was concentrating on her pleasure instead of being impatient for his own. No one had ever done that. He stopped and she moaned before touching her lips gently to his. When she pulled away, her eyes found his and she saw the need in them. Saw what she'd wanted to see in his eyes since she met him. Possession. Want. Need. So this is what 'just sex' felt like? Why hadn't she done this before? Why had she thought love was the answer? Cash didn't love her—he just wanted to make her feel good and she did. He moved his fingers, sliding up and down until he found the hard nub. She rubbed herself against him, gripping his forearm with her fingers and moving against him, her breath coming faster and harder.

'You're beautiful,' he whispered as he watched her. 'I want to see you come.'

The pressure built and she moved and moaned until nothing else existed except for him and her and the feeling of pure pleasure as his fingers moved against her, inside her and around her. Her body rose as the pleasure built until everything went black and time stood still and she came against his fingers.

She moaned and the pleasure returned in waves as aftershocks rocked her body.

'Faith.' His voice was rough and he kept his hand still as she moved and shifted, allowing her body to come back down from the high he'd just given her.

He fluttered light kisses against her eyelids and at the corner of her mouth, then he stilled, his forehead leaning against hers.

Faith's chest felt as if it were going to burst. She'd never... never experienced that with any man before. She'd never had someone focus on her so intently. Never had someone so determined to make sure she was satisfied. Everything felt different. Everything looked brighter but as the sound of the waves became louder and Cash kissed her again something changed. His eyes met hers and he gave her that look. The one that made her think things that weren't real. The satisfying pounding in her chest became more fluttery. Heat rose up her chest and into her cheeks.

'Faith?' he asked, his hand coming up to her face. 'What's wrong?'

'Nothing.'

'Bull. I can tell when you're lying, you know. Didn't you enjoy that?'

'Yes, yes, I did. Very much. It's just...'

'What?' His voice was gentle and it was making her heart beat even faster. She knew she couldn't do this.

'Nothing. Just hold me.' And he did. Faith burrowed her head into his shoulder and he wrapped his strong arms around her and held on tight until the ridiculous feeling in her heart started to subside and the water taxi arrived to take them home.

CHAPTER TWENTY

FAITH'S APARTMENT WASN'T far from the dock. He kept his hands to himself as they walked and Faith's fears grew. What if that was it? What if he'd realised this was a bad idea? She wasn't ready to let him go yet—she wanted more. She wanted him to show her more.

The security code on her door didn't work. She let out a frustrated sigh and tried again but it refused to work. She tried again but at that moment, Cash moved forward. His big, warm body covered her back and she felt him up against her—hard and ready. When his hands lifted her hair and his lips fell onto the back of her neck she wondered whether her next orgasm would last till she got to the bedroom. She'd never been on such alert. But his hand came up to her shoulder and slid down her arm and his deep voice growled in her ear, 'What's the number? I'll do it.'

'It's fine. I have it.' She twisted her body and punched in the number and to her relief the door buzzed and she fell in, moving quickly to punch the elevator button. She punched it again. And again. Cash stayed silent, standing at a distance with his hands casually in his pockets.

The lift seemed to take years but it finally came and she stepped in. When he followed all the oxygen seemed to disappear. They travelled in silence for a few floors before she heard him let out a sigh.

'Are you all right? Have you changed your mind?'

'No!' She schooled her voice as she gripped her bag and coat harder in her hands. 'No.' Planting a smile on her face, she moved until she was right in front of him. He didn't move, just stared down at her, his hands still in his pockets.

'I haven't changed my mind, have you?'

He paused for a second, his eyes searching her face. 'No.'

The lift pinged and Faith moved to the door quickly. Her heart was beating frantically. That familiar feeling of there being something more between them was returning but she had to hold it back. This was just sex. He didn't want anything more and what she needed was to get through this. To stop wanting more because that was her problem. She always wanted more. She just had to do this—get it done and over before she thought too much. As soon as the door swung open she dropped her bag and coat and reached for him. Her lips landed on his and he responded, grabbing her shoulders and kissing her back deep and hard. She pushed into him, making his back bang against the wall, and his hands moved to her hips. She could feel the bone in his hip against her torso and the long, hard length of him pressed against her. She reached out and gripped him through his trousers, feeling the heat of his penis through the fabric. Immediately his hand came out and grasped her wrist stopping her long strokes.

'I think we need to slow down.' His voice was deeper than before and it turned her on even more.

'No, this is about sex and I just want to have sex. With you,' she said as her desire overcame her thoughts. She wanted him. Naked and underneath her. On top of her. All over her and she couldn't wait.

She wasn't sure where he kissed her. On the mouth, on the eyes, on the neck. His lips were everywhere and his hands removed every inch of her clothing before she knew what was happening. She wanted him naked too. She wanted his hot skin against hers but he stopped and held both her hands. She tried to push back into him, tried to kiss him again but he stopped her—pushing her away easily and twisting her hands behind her back.

'Wait,' he said quietly.

She waited, her chest heaving and her breathing ragged. What was he waiting for? Had he changed his mind? Was he going to leave?

'Let me look at you.'

His words startled her. Look at her? They were in the middle of the most erotic kissing session she'd ever experienced and he wanted to look at her? She didn't want him to look, she just wanted to do this before she thought too much. Before she started to fall for him because she knew her heart wouldn't take that pain.

'Look at me in here.' She tried to pull his hands and lead him into the bedroom but he didn't budge.

'Wait. Not so fast.' He pulled her back and his eyes roved her face. Then they slid down her body before one of his hands let go of hers and he lifted it to her collarbone. With surprising reverence he ran his fingers across the long bone at the base of her neck. Then he dipped his head and kissed her right at the base of her throat. She was wetter than ever. And swollen and throbbing and she wanted him to get on with it. But he didn't. His fingers trailed even further down her chest, in between her breasts, before he cupped the left one in his palm.

'Beautiful,' he murmured before leaning down and taking her nipple in his mouth. Faith wanted to cry, she wanted to explode, but she didn't. She moaned. Uncontrollably. Her hands moved to the back of his head as his tongue flicked over her nipple, back and forth and around until she felt the bones in her knees give. But he didn't stop—he just used his free arm to wrap around her waist and lift her up.

This wasn't how it was supposed to happen. It was supposed to be hard and fast and she wasn't supposed to feel anything. Then she could go back to the way it was. She could forget about him and it would be over. But so far—

everything he was doing was making her think more and more that this was something more. That this was real. But it wasn't.

She gripped the hair on the back of his head and pulled, violently. 'Stop that.'

He looked up in surprise and let her feet drop back down onto the ground. 'Was I hurting you?'

'No. You weren't. But I don't want you to do that.'

She pushed him away, angry but not sure why. His brow furrowed as she stepped back.

She tried to control her breathing, she tried to relieve the ache in her chest but while she looked at him she couldn't. She felt a breeze pass by her naked body. She'd been out of control. She couldn't let that happen. She needed to be in charge.

'Follow me,' she said, and kicked her heels off before padding into her bedroom. Pulling the curtains shut, she ordered him onto the bed. 'Wait there.'

She went into her walk-in wardrobe and reached out for the velvet-covered ottoman before sitting down, her legs shaking and her heart still beating like a bongo drum. She lifted a hand to her forehead. She had to calm down. Stay in control.

She had to think of something. Her eyes searched the small space until they landed on a silk suit hanger. A gift from Betty when she recorded her first story about bur-lesque. Perfect. It was just what she needed to stop thinking that this was more than just sex.

CHAPTER TWENTY-ONE

CASH FOUGHT HARD to control the beating in his chest and he fought hard to ignore the uncomfortable tightness in his pants. Faith was beautiful. Even more gorgeous than he'd imagined, and she was hot for him. Out of control. The noises she made and the taste of her skin on his tongue made his brain spiral. All he could think of was her. And he wanted her back in here. Not in there, doing God only knew what. Applying perfume? Shaving her legs? Who knew? But he didn't care. He wanted her back in here, her small soft body against his. Now.

He took a second to look around. Her bedroom was filled with stuff. Jewellery, clothes, perfume, shoes. Things hung on lampshades but her bed was unusually spare. There were two white pillows and the rest of the linen was white. He liked it. As if this bed was all about the two people who were about to be in it. Nothing else. Just her and him. Naked.

He kicked his shoes off and lay back on the bed, breathing in her scent that lingered on the bedclothes. It made him twitch again. He couldn't get the way she reacted to him out of his mind. She wanted him as much as he wanted her and that made something grow bigger inside him. And not just what was between his legs. He'd been with women who wanted him before but Faith was different. She was desperate for him. And he was desperate to see her again.

A voice hammered in his brain. The one that told him this

wouldn't end well. The one that reminded him that this was supposed to be just sex. But he ignored it. He wanted her in his arms. Was desperate for her. The way she was desperate for him. Doubts crept into the corners of his mind. He couldn't want her too much. He couldn't let her have that power over him. He didn't want to fall for her.

A few seconds passed before the door of the room she'd escaped to opened and his breath stopped in his throat. She'd let her hair down and it floated over her shoulders. She raised her hands up to either side of the door frame and was smiling at him, a wicked, playful smile that was making him throb. She was dressed in a black string bikini-type thing, wearing the bra he'd caught a glimpse of last week in the boardroom. Two bows covered her nipples and one covered the place between her legs. The place he wanted to get to. The place he wanted to kiss and suck and lave. A moment ago she'd been naked and now she was covered up. His eyes ventured back to her face and he throbbed even harder.

'How do you like this?' she asked, her voice innocent but her body looking anything but.

'I'd like it off.'

'Patience…' She stepped towards him, her hips swinging, and looped her thumbs in between the black strings surrounding her breasts and her skin.

He waited. Surely she'd slip that thing off soon. He wanted what was underneath. He wanted to kiss her skin, not the strings of this outfit.

'Good things come to those who wait,' she scolded when he reached for her.

She turned her back to him and swung her hips—much as the stripper on stage had. It fired his blood. She had a beautiful arse. Round and firm and high. He wanted to touch it but she was just out of reach.

Her hands came around to unhook the contraption at the back and he let out a breath when she turned. But those bows were still there, hiding what he wanted to see.

'Sex isn't all about the act itself. It's about anticipation...'
Her voice was breathy and it was making him even harder.
She still swayed and moved but her eyes were set directly
on his. He couldn't wait much longer. If she didn't get this
stuff off, he'd reach for her. Grab her and throw her on the
bed. Then he'd kiss her all over.

'I've been anticipating this all day.'

'You have?' She raised an eyebrow.

'Yes.'

'Why?'

This wasn't what he wanted. He didn't want to talk. He
wanted to kiss and touch and plunge himself into her. He
drew himself up and reached for her and she didn't resist.
He spread his hands around her hips and kneeled up, drawing her body to him.

'You fascinate me, Faith. You're interesting and fiery and
strong, but soft and vulnerable and I want to know more.'

'More?'

'More. I want to know everything. Take this off. I want to
see you.' He leaned forward and kissed her neck. She liked
that. She shivered every time he did it. He wanted her to
shiver. He wanted her to whimper as she had earlier. Then
he wanted her to scream out. Preferably his name, over and
over till she disturbed the neighbours and they called the po-
lice. He wanted this to just be sex but the more she talked,
the deeper he was falling. His hands moved down her body
and slid in behind the strings of her complicated underwear
but she moved away.

'You don't like this?'

'I do like this. It's sexy but...unnecessary. I want to see
your body. I want to see the curve of your stomach and the
way your breasts bounce. I want to touch you, feel how wet
you are. I want to kiss your skin. I want to know you, Faith.'

Her eyes met his and locked. 'Cash...don't say that.' She'd
gone quiet and stiff. He moved his hands up and rested them

on her shoulders. She was upset. He could feel it and he didn't know why.

'What is it?' he asked quietly, tilting his head to look into her eyes. If he could see her eyes, he'd know what she was feeling. Her eyes never lied. 'What did I say?'

Her eyes went hard. Something changed. This wasn't Faith. She was thinking again. 'Faith?'

'Stop talking,' she said, and she pushed her hands into his chest. 'Sit,' she ordered as he fell back. She took the opportunity to shuffle closer until she was on top of him, straddling him. She grabbed at his belt buckle.

'Whoa. Hang on. I want this to last.'

'No!' Her voice was angry, terse. She ripped at the bows still on her nipples and threw them onto the floor. 'That's not what this is about.'

She tugged at his pants again. Her desperation was turning him on. He was rock hard and he helped her ease his jeans down his legs. But she didn't even wait to take them off. She reached into his boxer shorts and pulled his penis out, holding it in her hand.

'Faith,' he murmured, trying to still her hand as she stroked him. 'Slower...slower. I want to last.'

She licked at his neck and kissed him. Then she bit him and his whole body spasmed. She was horny as hell and hot for him and he wanted her. Bad.

She pushed herself down onto him and his mind went blank for a moment, enjoying the warmth of her as she wriggled against him impatiently.

'Maybe we should try some of that tantric we learned at Patricia's,' he murmured, trying to distract her. Trying to get her to slow down. If she kept going like this he wasn't going to last long at all and he wanted this to last all night.

But before she even had a chance to answer she'd produced a condom from nowhere, slipped it over his quivering cock, lifted herself up, pushed aside her small panties and slid onto him.

He groaned and gripped the bed. She lifted herself up again and slid down. He held on tight. She was hot and wet and moving so fast his mind was about to burst.

'Stop, Faith…slow down.' He grabbed her arm to hold her still but she threw it off. Her breasts rubbed against his stubble. He tried to take a nipple in his mouth—he wanted her to feel this everywhere—but she moved away.

'Don't kiss me—just do me,' she demanded.

He didn't want to do it like this. He wanted it to last, but her dirty words and her insistence had him aching for release. She pumped him faster and he encouraged her. He forgot to think; all he could do now was feel. Her. Hot and wet and surrounding him. Sucking him and making him blow. Which he did no more than a minute later.

The blood rushed from his groin to his head and he waited until the throbbing subsided.

She tried to push up and off him but he held her still. He wasn't letting her go. This wasn't how it was supposed to be.

'What the hell was that?'

'Sex.' She was panting and he opened his eyes to see her wide eyed and red cheeked. Beautiful. Hot. But not sated. Not even close.

'That was fantastic,' he said with a groan.

She stared at him, her eyes even wider and glassier. He didn't know what to say. She was disappointed. He'd done what she'd thought he would. Just sex. But he hadn't wanted to do that. He'd wanted more. So much more.

'Faith? Just give me a minute. I'll be ready again in a minute.' His whole body was limp. He felt boneless but he could go again. He knew he'd only have to kiss her for a few minutes and he could go again. Give her what she needed.

Faith shifted. She moved up and slipped off him. She pushed him away when he reached for her, and righted her underwear. Cash wanted to hold her, he wanted to give her more but she stepped back—out of his reach. He stood and cleaned himself up and she stood watching. It felt cold and awkward and Cash's stomach clamped. This wasn't what he wanted. It wasn't supposed to be like this.

CHAPTER TWENTY-TWO

'FAITH...' CASH REACHED for her but she stepped away.

'It's all right, Cash, you were right.' She found herself a short silk robe and slid it over her shoulders. 'Sex can be just sex.'

But that wasn't what he wanted. He wanted more. He reached for her again but she was too fast.

'I think you should leave now.'

'I'm not going anywhere until you tell me what's wrong. What was that? Why don't you want to do this properly?'

'Did I do it wrong?' She turned to him, her arms folded and her mouth set in an angry line.

'No.' He tried to reach for her again but she moved even further away, out of his reach. 'Faith, you didn't do anything wrong, but you didn't finish. I want you to finish.'

'Why? What difference does it make? It was just sex.'

Just sex. Those were his words. He'd wanted this. He'd wanted this to be just a night of hot sex, but now he didn't know what he wanted.

'You're angry.'

'I'm not angry.'

She was angry. 'I understand how you're feeling. I get it, Faith.' He did get it. She'd really wanted to believe this would be more. That was why she was so angry.

Faith closed her eyes and turned her head. She hated him. He could see that.

'Just go, Cash.' Her voice sounded strangely calm and it made him want to hold her, but she had her arms wound tight and she wasn't letting him in. It took a few seconds and a sharp pain in his chest to realise this wasn't about her show. This was about how she felt. She'd trusted him and he'd let her down and now she didn't trust him anymore. She didn't believe in him and she definitely didn't believe in love.

'Faith…'

'Go. It was just sex.' This time her eyes set on his. They didn't blink. They looked at him intently and he knew they were telling the truth. For her—this had just been sex. He stepped back and scooped his clothes up, all the while keeping his eyes on hers. Watching for any sign that this was more than sex. Any sign that she wanted him to stay. But her eyes remained unmoving and her arms still folded across her chest. That was it. Done. They'd had sex. And it was just sex. He should feel better. He should feel how he normally did when he just had sex. But he didn't. He felt as if someone had reached into his chest, ripped out his beating heart and thrown it against the wall. Which frightened the hell out of him, so he did the only thing he could think of to do. He left.

So that was it. That was what 'just sex' felt like. Faith was finishing up her voice-overs. She kept making mistakes. She kept saying the wrong thing and repeating herself and she kept going over and over the footage that the camera had captured at the burlesque. Where Cash was talking to her. Where he was kissing her neck.

She had to stop doing this to herself. It was over. And she'd been at this for seven hours. She was tired and frustrated and she wanted to go home. At least she wouldn't run into Cash out here in the studio. He never came out here. Only the sound guys and the cameramen and the producers came out here and luckily they were all busy today and she was alone.

'Sexual fantasies are just that. Some women don't need

them to be real for them to be powerful—just the thought of them is enough.' She listened to her voice play back over the tape. 'But for others—they're as necessary as air, as water. So next time you catch your girlfriend yawning as you assume the missionary position—allow her to live out her fantasies and get ready for the hottest sex of your life.'

'Perfect. Although I'd probably add in a joke at the end. A joke always makes a man feel more comfortable.'

The voice she'd been dreading sounded from the door behind her. He was here and she couldn't turn around. She wouldn't. She didn't want to see him. Or talk to him. Or think about him because in that moment she knew; she knew she'd been right all along. Sex was never just sex.

'I was just leaving.' She gathered up the papers she had strewn across the sound board. She'd written and rewritten the script so many times there were dozens of pages lying around.

'Wait. I want to see how the show ended up.'

'You'll see it in a few hours when it goes to air.' Her skin prickled as he sat in the chair next to her. Still she didn't look at him. Couldn't look at him. Just the scent of him was too much. Her stomach rolled and she tugged her sleeves up at the immediate heat that spread throughout her body. She remembered last night. The way she'd thrown herself onto him. She didn't wait. She didn't listen; she just kept going and going until he couldn't stop.

'I'd like to see it now.'

Finally she looked at him and his eyes hit her as she knew they would. But she went on regardless. 'Fine, look at it. Go through it. It's my last one. You were right. Sex is just sex. I'll pack up my desk and be gone within the hour.' But as she stood to leave he grabbed her. His strength always surprised her but right now he was even stronger than ever. He pulled her quickly and expertly into his lap.

'You're not going anywhere.' He was so close now, his

lips tempting her. His breath hot on her mouth. A rage of hot need sang through her and she wanted him all over again.

'Let me go.'

'No. I won't. Not until you tell me what the hell happened last night.'

'We had sex.'

'Yes, we did. But there was more to it than that.'

'No, there wasn't. It was just sex.' She didn't want to be here. She didn't want to be sitting on his lap and feeling him hard beneath her and she definitely didn't want to look into his eyes. Those beautiful dark eyes that seemed to look right into her and see her for who she really was.

'You were upset and angry and I want to know why.' His arms slackened so she used the opportunity to stand up. She couldn't be near him; she didn't want to be with him—just as he didn't want to be with her.

'Last night was a mistake. I let you do something I shouldn't have.'

'You let me in.'

'No. I didn't. I let you have sex and I shouldn't have.'

He stood up and moved closer and Faith held steady. *Never let them see you cry,* she remembered. *Don't show them emotion.* But for some reason she wanted him to see. She wanted him to see her and catch her, but he wouldn't. She knew he wouldn't.

'What happened?' he asked, his voice so gentle and deep it disturbed her pulse.

'What do you mean?'

'What happened?'

What happened? He wanted to know what happened? She'd lost it, that was what, which was what she felt like doing right now. 'You want to know what happened? I have no idea if sex is just sex or something more because I know nothing about sex. I'm no expert, I barely know what I'm doing and last night I got everything wrong. I always get everything wrong.'

CHAPTER TWENTY-THREE

CASH STARED AT the emotional woman in front of him. His stomach had been rolling all day. He felt sick every time he thought about what she'd said when he left. *It was just sex.* But she'd been so desperate and seemed to want it over so fast. And then she'd been so distant and emotional when it was over. A panicked thought grasped his brain.

'Faith—are you… Have you… How many times have you had sex?'

Faith's face fell.

'You know, don't you? You realised last night. Three. That's my number. Three. And I've never had an orgasm. Never…before…you. At the dock. I have no idea what I'm doing.'

Cash watched her in stunned silence. Sydney's sexpert had been with only three men? Faith? The hottest women he'd ever met had never had an orgasm? But she had, with him. A crazy feeling of possession grasped at him. That she was his. Her shoulders shook so he reached for her. Pulling himself up next to her, he wrapped his arms around her and pulled her head to his shoulder.

'Faith, it makes no difference how many times you've done it. Last night, that was hot. You're hot. You did everything right.'

Her eyes met his. Challenging. Not letting go. 'No, it was…just sex.'

'That wasn't "just" anything. That was amazing. You're amazing.'

'Cash, don't say that. You don't know. What I am...who I am. I have absolutely no idea what I'm doing. I'm no sexpert. I'm a sexflop.'

Cash leaned down to kiss her forehead. 'What you are is sexperfect.'

He watched her and she watched him back. Then she smiled and let out a little laugh.

'That's not even a word.'

'Neither is sexflop.'

Faith became aware of his arm around her. She liked the feel of it—warm and comforting. As if she belonged. As if she were his. She snuggled in a little closer.

'Cash, I can't help it.'

'Can't help what?'

'Thinking sex is about more than just sex.'

He hesitated, then she felt his hand on her jaw, moving her face to meet his eyes.

'Maybe you're right.' He kissed her eyes and she closed them briefly before meeting his gaze. 'With you, sex could never be just sex.'

He felt her still beneath him.

'Wasn't that...just sex...for you?' she asked, her voice shaking a little.

He'd tried to stay away, he'd tried to resist her, but he wanted her and he didn't care if it hurt. He had to have more.

'No.'

'No?'

'No. That was more than just sex. That was...' What was it? He couldn't even begin to figure it out. All he knew was that he wanted more. He wanted her. 'Something.'

'Something?'

'Something.'

Cash sat back in his chair before lifting his hands to her

waist and placing a big hand either side of her, pulling her closer and pressing his lips to her stomach.

'You once asked me why I did this, Cash, why I researched sex and love and relationships. It's because I don't know anything about it. No one has ever wanted that from me. I left home when I was seven. I never fitted in at boarding school—the other girls would push me and tease me and I learned to be small. I learned to disappear—but after...'

She stopped so he kissed her again. He wanted to know more. He wanted to know why she acted so tough and as if she needed no one, because he wanted her to need him. 'After I made a mistake and slept with that teacher, I decided I didn't want to be small any more. I wanted to matter. To someone. I needed to know how. I wanted to know what it felt like to be loved and how to have an orgasm and what it's like when someone makes love to you. I don't want just sex. I've never wanted just sex. I want more.'

Cash hesitated. She wanted more. Could he really give her more? Could he really make her happy? He wasn't sure but as he looked up at her he knew that he had to try. He had to trust her.

'I want to make love to you, Faith. I want more.'

Faith's heart swelled. She knew she shouldn't let it but it did anyway. His voice was deep and vibrated through her skin and his hands held her steady. Did he really mean it or was this just about sex again? She wanted to believe him. She wanted to let him in but after he left last night it had hurt so much.

Carefully she leaned down and touched her lips to his. They parted and he let her in, waiting for her to let him know when she was ready for more. Her hands smoothed over his hair and settled around his neck. His hands held tighter around her waist and he pulled her even closer.

'How about I come and see you tonight? We can watch your show together.'

She wanted that. She wanted him—but what then? He

was cancelling her show. Would he feel obligated to keep it on now even if he didn't want it? She didn't want that. She wanted him for no other reason than he wanted her.

'I'll take the job.'

'What?' He pushed her back a little and stared up at her, confusion on his face.

'On the breakfast programme. If you can't make my show work, I'll take the presenter's job.'

'Why?'

'Because there's something I want more than recognition and awards.' He blinked and she hesitated. Her heart felt raw and open and she wondered if she was doing the right thing. 'You.' There. She'd said it. Her heart was open to him. She was bare and now he could hurt her more than ever.

He pulled her towards him and kissed her stomach again. 'Good. Because I want you.'

CHAPTER TWENTY-FOUR

THAT NIGHT FAITH changed her outfit seven times. She poured some wine then put it back in the bottle. Too obvious. She turned off the light and lit the lamps. Too dark. She turned the lights back on again. No, then he'd see the pimple that had formed in the last hour on her chin. Her palms were damp and her hair wouldn't sit right but when her buzzer rang she knew there was no more time left. He was here. And he wanted her.

He greeted her with a kiss on the cheek but she'd gone for his lips and they mashed together somewhere near her eye. She giggled and he laughed and they said nothing as she led him into the living room and turned on the television.

'Wine?' she asked. He nodded and she left to pour the glasses again.

She wasn't sure why she was so nervous. They'd done this already. They'd seen each other naked. They'd kissed each other so many times she knew exactly where he liked to be kissed. On the neck, just below his ear. But her hands shook as she poured the red liquid into the oversized glass. Because this meant more. He'd agreed. This wasn't just sex. This was more.

'Has it started yet?'

The music that indicated the start of her show sang through the nervous atmosphere and Cash reached for the remote to turn it up. A comfortable feeling enveloped Faith's body. She curled her legs up and shifted until her shoulder was against his. His arm came down and around her shoulder and she sat still. Not wanting to move an inch. Not wanting to break whatever this fragile link between them was. She had to be cool, calm. She couldn't want this so much because if she did—she was sure she'd stuff it up.

'Fantasies. We've all got them. Some dream of winning the lottery, others of playing sport for our country…' Faith heard Cash's snigger as a flash of Faith dressed in cricket pads flashed on the screen. Faith winced. She really did some ridiculous things for this show. 'But there are some fantasies all of us have but most are too afraid to share.' The scene changed to Kitty's dungeon. Faith's shoulders twitched. Their first kiss was in that dungeon. He'd dominated her in that dungeon and she'd dominated him. Faith tried to breathe normally. Cool. Calm. 'Sexual fantasies.'

The show went on. Cash laughed in all the right places. He went quiet when he should and when the scene of her dressed in the schoolgirl outfit came on his large hand settled protectively over her thigh. Comfort. Protection. Understanding. Faith felt her heart swell and her eyes itch. *Don't push it,* she reminded herself. *Don't show him how much you care.* She'd learned that the hard way. When she let the group of day-girls at her school see how much she loved the comfort pack her mother had sent. It was the first one she'd ever received and it had had all her favourite things in it. A *Sweet Valley High* book, a packet of McVities and a letter from her mother. Those girls had pushed her until she'd dropped the parcel, laughed as they'd read the letter out loud, eaten all her biscuits and stolen her book. *Don't show them how much you care.*

The credits rolled as the show ended and Cash heard Faith suck in a deep breath before finally she turned his way till their eyes locked. Brown eyes locked with blue. The land meeting the ocean. Her eyes were beautiful. They'd held him prisoner since the day he first tried to cancel her show. They were the eyes of someone who couldn't be held down—who couldn't stay still. Faith was someone always searching for answers and tonight's show was no different. Funny, irreverent, insightful. He was an idiot to think her show couldn't work. She just needed more help—more direction.

It was as if he'd been living in the shadows and suddenly they'd cleared. He needed to tell her. Grant had called today. But he didn't want to tell her; he didn't want her to know. Not yet. Not while he had her here. Needing him. It felt so good, so right and he wanted it to last. At least one more night. Tomorrow this could be all over but he had tonight and even if it broke him he'd show her how he felt and that she mattered to him. Always had.

'So, what did you think?' She looked nervous. He pulled her in tighter. He knew why she doubted herself, because he hadn't shown her any faith.

'It was…' she looked up at him in anticipation '…brilliant.'

Her smile spread slowly and he leaned in to kiss it. He wanted to kiss her all over but she pulled away. 'Didn't I tell you I was brilliant?'

'No, you didn't. But you are. Brilliant and beautiful.'

'You've finally seen the light.' She laughed and his chest hurt. She had no idea.

'You shouldn't be doing it all on your own.'

Her smile faltered and she went a little stiff. 'It doesn't matter now.'

He wanted to tell her it did. He wanted to tell her he'd changed his mind, but if he did she'd think he was only saying that because he wanted sex and that wasn't true so he didn't say anything. His urge to speak up and be honest about that lay still and coiled deep within him. But he could be honest about something else.

'You know what matters? This. You. Us. Right now. Here. This matters. You matter. To me.'

Her eyes locked with his and he felt it. Burning. Heating. A look that crept slowly through his eyes and hurt his chest.

'And you matter to me,' she whispered. Before she could say another word Cash reached for her. He lowered her until he was lying on top of her on the lounge and his lips shifted to her mouth, where he kissed her firmly and eagerly. His mouth moved to her neck and she let out a whimper of pleasure and pushed herself into him—wanting him close, needing to feel his hardness and strength. Needing her to believe that he wanted her.

'So you think the show was good.'

'It was perfect.'

'So which fantasy did you like best?'

He met her eyes. 'I have the only fantasy I need right here, in my arms.'

Cash kissed her. Over and over and over. Kissed her until she couldn't breathe. But he didn't go any further. Faith knew he was holding back. And she knew why. He was making love to her; this wasn't just sex. He was giving her everything she'd ever wanted and as she felt his hands move through her hair and over her shoulders she knew what she wanted. To be with him.

Slowly and deliberately he lifted her fingers to his lips and with his eyes still on hers he kissed them. A slow, sluggish pleasure ran through her as if he'd released a drug into her system. Warm fog enveloped her mind and her body became boneless. She pushed on his chest.

'I want to go to the bedroom.' He smiled but she didn't. This wasn't sex. This was so much more and she wasn't sure if she could go through with this. But he got up and held out his hand for her to take as she stood.

'Tonight we go slower,' he said, leaning down to kiss her. One side of his mouth turned up in a small smile and she finally smiled back at him.

'OK.'

'Tonight I want you to enjoy it as much as I do.'

This wasn't just sex; it never would be. Tonight she was going to have sex with him to prove to herself that sex wasn't just sex and that there was something between them. And that she mattered.

'Then you better get started.' Faith smiled as he walked her into the room. Nervously, she lay on the bed but her stomach settled when he lay down next to her. He let his finger move over her eyebrow and down her cheek.

'Are you sure this is what you want?' His voice was gruff and quiet and laced with a rawness that made her shiver.

'Yes.' A simple answer. An unfamiliar clarity that pierced her brain, her heart and her soul. Yes.

He held her hand still until she met his eyes.

'I want to know you, Faith.' His words were gentle and made her hesitate. He wanted to know her. He wanted to see her. This wasn't an act, this was real and she wasn't sure if she was prepared. 'Even if this doesn't work out, I want to know you.'

She heard the hesitation in his voice. Like her, he was unsure of what this was. Whether it was anything, but she had to find out.

'I'm not easy to get to know.'

'Yes, you are. I can read you like a book and I know you're scared.'

Faith shivered at the way he'd read her thoughts. 'I just want this, Cash. I just want to enjoy this. Just this.'

He cocked an eyebrow and she waited, holding her breath. She still wasn't sure what he wanted.

'And I want to seduce you.'

A wide smile planted itself on her face and she knew it probably wasn't very sexy but she left it there as she struggled to unbutton his shirt. Her hands were shaking a little. She shifted and moved closer, then shifted again, moving on top of him, then slipping off again.

He laughed and gripped her by the waist. 'You're not terribly good at this seduction caper, are you?'

She couldn't help but laugh back. 'I'm a little out of practice.'

He lifted his hands and put them either side of her face. That simple movement made her feel vulnerable and small. She lifted her hands to cover his. She wanted to be in charge but with his large hands either side of her face she felt his attention again. His focus. It made her feel as if she was under his power. But his whispered words soothed her.

'Let me make love to you, Faith.'

Her chest was full and she didn't know what to say. No one had ever said that to her before. She'd never felt more important.

Panic spread across her. He seemed so intent, so focused. 'Are you sure we should be doing this?'

His eyes were dark. 'Yes.' No indecision laced his words. Confident. Sure. He knew what he wanted and at the sound of that one word, with unfamiliar simplicity, so did she. He unbuttoned her top and let it slide off her shoulders, his eyes moving across her body as he did it. She could see his hunger. He wanted her. Really wanted her.

'You're gorgeous,' he said simply before pulling her up and on top of him and she felt him hard and ready against her. A sharp breath filled her lungs.

His face was hard and angular beneath her and she realised she wanted him to bare himself to her as she was doing to him. 'Make love to me, Cash.'

He shifted his hips until she tipped off him. Using his arms to hold her steady, he moved her expertly beneath him so he was hovering above her, one knee either side her. Then, before she could resist, he held her hands above her head. Faith gasped her approval.

'This is my fantasy, Faith. You.' His voice was a growl. An animalistic demand and she reacted to it instinctively, pushing her chest forward, her nipples responding to the hardness of his chest. He noticed her impatience and dipped his head to kiss her neck. He breathed her in and it made her feel as if he was using every opportunity to remember her. As if there was nothing else but him and her and he wanted to experience all of it. Her heart beat faster in her chest. *Stay calm,* she schooled herself. *You won't fall. He won't hurt you. You can let him in; you can let him know. You will be fine.*

'Please, Cash.' Her voice shook a little.

His lips trailed from underneath her ear to her shoulder and he nipped at her skin through the thin fabric of the shirt she was wearing. She shivered in coiled anticipation. He was in no hurry and she didn't want him to be. She wanted this to last for ever.

'Do you want me to beg?' she asked. He looked up at her from where he was kissing her shoulder and smiled the most decadent, wicked smile she'd seen on his lips yet.

'No. I want you to enjoy it.' His hands moved to her bra and he pulled it aside to pay attention to her now aching breasts. She sighed gratefully as he unclipped it and pulled it off her hot skin and off her body. Then he pulled down her jeans and the small black panties she had on before she reached up to unbutton his shirt.

He stood and she watched as he slipped the stiff shirt off over his head, most of the buttons still intact. His shoulders were wide and the muscles in them corded and straining. Hard, powerful, golden shoulders. Broad shoulders that could take anything. His lips fell hungrily to her skin. He kissed down her neck and to her breast, where he paused before taking the hard bud in his mouth. Licking and sucking until she wanted to scream out. She put both her hands on the back of his head to keep him where he was and moaned in appreciation of his efforts. He stood again to slip off his jeans and boxers and she watched him jutting out hard and ready and she wanted him more than ever.

She was naked now and more exposed to him than she'd ever been to anyone. The light was still on so she could see everything that was happening. Somehow that turned her on even more. Her being exposed to him and him to her like this was exhilarating and strangely freeing. She could see him and she wanted him to see her. She wanted to keep the memory of this night in her mind for ever.

His fingertips grazed her skin as they moved lazily down her body to find the soft skin of her inner thigh.

'Cash…' The word was a warning, but she wasn't sure what of. Only that with every touch she fell deeper and deeper under his control.

She bucked and shivered and his mouth moved into a smile at her breast. He flicked his eyes back up to hers as he continued to kiss down her body all the while his fingers drew lazy circles on her thigh. She tried to grip his hair but it was too short so she gripped the bed instead.

'I need to know what you like.' His voice, raw and needy, vibrated through her stomach where he was kissing her just above her navel.

'I like this. I like everything you do,' she tried to say but her voice was slightly strangled.

He kissed her again, across her ribs and down to the soft mound of her belly. Then his other hand came up and his thumb traced a line right to her most swollen and sensitive centre and she bucked again, throwing her head back.

'I can't promise I'll be gentle, not when you make noises like that.' He paused and watched her before pressing a gentle kiss right where his thumb had been and Faith called out.

'Don't be gentle,' she begged.

The air changed. Everything that had been slow and careful was now fast and furious. He slid his body up until he reached her mouth and kissed her hard. She met his aggression and put her hands behind his head, drawing him closer. Faith moved her hands down to his stomach and traced her fingers over his muscles before looking down to see him hard and free and proud. She took him in. All of him. Every silky, thick, long inch of him and lust licked all around her. His eyes devoured her body as she watched him and he fell on top of her again, kissing and licking and rubbing his hands over the place his lips were about to touch. His mouth teased and tempted until she couldn't wait any longer.

'Wait. Condom.'

Cash seemed to come out of a daze at her comment, but he stopped.

'I don't...'

'A sex journalist should be prepared for any situation.' She smiled as she slid from underneath him to race inside and retrieve the box from the drawer next to her bed. She'd got it out of a goodie bag from Sexpo, which she covered on her website last year. *Thank God for Sexpo.*

She leaned back and resumed her position before ripping the foil open with her teeth. Cash stopped to watch. He reached out to take it from her but she pulled her hands away.

'Uh-uh. I get to do this.' But her smile faded when a bright fluoro-green condom slipped out of the pack. He raised an eyebrow and her stomach flipped at the sight of it, but she didn't care what colour the condom was. She needed him inside her. Now.

Sucking her bottom lip in between her teeth, she placed the condom on the tip of him. He was big. Bigger than anyone she'd ever seen, satiny smooth skin over hard steel. Just looking at it was making all the blood in her body rush right to her core. Slowly and carefully she unravelled the bright green condom, letting her fingers caress him as she pushed the protection down. A hiss escaped from Cash's lips and she barely got to the bottom when he fell on top of her, pushing her hands away.

The smile had disappeared from his lovely mouth and he ran his eyes up her body to hers.

'We do this slowly this time and you come first.' Then he moved his hot body over her, his skin hot against hers, positioning himself above her, the bright green tip of him pressing at her core. She pushed her hips up, begging, trying to get what she needed.

'Easy now,' he rumbled and he eased himself closer. She hadn't had time before to notice anything but now she noticed everything. The way his eyes had gone darker. The way his voice was lower and scraped across her skin. The way his skin felt, smooth and hot—his hard muscles tense against her. His mouth caught hers in an all-consuming kiss and she breathed in every essence of him. The masculine scent of his skin mingled with the tang of his cologne, the hardness of his muscles in his back against her fingers and the thickness of him as he eased himself closer were making her shiver.

'Wait.' She had to push on his chest. He stilled. He wasn't in a rush. He was giving her time to get used to his size and he waited, his hands either side of her. She ran her hands over the backs of his arms, feeling the tense muscles.

'Give me a second,' she breathed.

'Concentrate.' His deep voice was laced with command and she looked up at him. He moved one hand to her belly and stroked before moving further down to find the hard nub that was now throbbing. He let his fingers work in lazy circles as she moved her hips, closing her eyes and letting her tongue trace her upper lip. He moved closer and she gasped, pushing her hands into his chest again so he stopped as she adjusted to the fullness she'd just taken before without appreciating.

'I'm ready.'

With an uncontrollable smile she relaxed and he pushed further. He moved slowly and easily rocking and thrusting until he drove her to the point where pleasure became pain and pain became pleasure and she burst. She gripped his back and pulled him closer and he answered, thrusting harder and faster and giving her everything she wanted until the pressure built and expanded again and she peaked around him again.

Cash knew it would take every ounce of self-control to hold back. He watched her tongue as it licked against her top lip and her eyes as they closed as if lost. Then she opened them and focused on him again and holding back became harder. She moved against him, lifting her hips to him and bringing him back down towards her and the heat in his body turned liquid. Then, when she came the second time and her fingernails scratched against his back he abandoned his control and let himself go, riding the invisible wave of madness with her.

When he opened his eyes he found her shivering in his arms. Her eyes met his and he watched her. Taking in the pink of her cheeks and the way her hair had unwound itself and was now spread across her shoulders. Her chest heaved and she clung to him, keeping her skin pressed against his. The steady beat of his heart was against her chest and he could feel the matching rhythm in hers. He wanted to remember everything about her. He wanted to remember the way she looked and the smell of her skin and the way she tasted because he knew she'd soon be gone and it would be over.

A throaty laugh escaped her mouth and his body heated at the sound of it. 'Now don't tell me that was just sex,' she said, her voice all breathy and ragged.

He opened his mouth to speak but nothing came out except a grunt. His shoulders shook as he strained to hold himself up and off her.

'What's that? The great Cash Anderson lost for words? That would be a first.'

He brought his hand around to her backside and pulled her closer to him. She gasped and he smiled down at her in satisfaction.

She looked up at him, all blue eyes and eyelashes. Her mouth came closer and those soft pink lips met his in a deep, alarmingly erotic kiss. His body responded the way it always did around this woman. It grew bigger, taller and stronger.

He pulled her even closer, wondering for a fleeting second how he was going to let her go.

'I don't always need to use words to express how I feel.'

She drew away and slid him a glance, her mouth spread in a satisfied smile. 'Then I think you better stop talking and do that again.'

CHAPTER TWENTY-FIVE

WHEN FAITH WOKE up Cash's big, heavy arm lay on her thigh. She could feel the tickle of his black hairs against her skin. It felt strange to wake up there in the arms of a man. She'd never taken a man back to her apartment. That had always been her place, her sanctuary, but Cash seemed so right there. But maybe this wasn't the greatest idea. Now that they'd done more than have 'just sex' she wondered how she was going to cope if this became more. A boyfriend. A proper boyfriend. She hadn't even considered that. What the hell did one do with a boyfriend?

Faith shifted a little, testing to see whether he was awake. But he said nothing and didn't move. She shifted again and reached for her phone that was sitting on the side table. She almost had it when he pushed against her. Hard and ready. Again. A strange warm feeling showered across her shoulders and down into her belly. He seemed to not be able to get enough of her and that made her feel good. As if he needed her. No one had ever needed her.

She needed to untangle herself, get into the shower and think.

Carefully she shifted her leg and pushed her body forward. Better to leave without waking him. She wasn't ready to face him yet. Wasn't ready to face what had happened between them. And she knew without any doubt that what they'd done last night definitely wasn't just sex. She managed to get one toe out before a large and heavy arm snaked around her waist.

'Morning.' Cash's sleepy, deep voice made her stop where she was.

'It's late. I need a shower.'

She tried to pull away but he pulled her in closer and kissed the back of her neck. Pinpricks of pleasure shot through her neck and down her spine. She closed her eyes and rolled her neck back, enjoying the warmth of his big body and those mind-numbing kisses.

Faith turned and looked at his face. His eyes were closed and he looked much younger lying there, comfortable between her white sheets.

'I can feel you looking at me, you know,' his deep, sleepy voice mumbled. Faith smiled. She needed to feel him again. She snuggled back down into the bed and he slung a large, warm arm around her before opening his eyes. His eyes were even more beautiful in the morning. Soft and sleepy, half open and fixed on her.

'Are you all right?' The tenderness in his voice surprised her. She met his steady gaze. He smiled and lifted his hand to rub a thumb over her eyebrow. 'Are you…feeling all right?'

'I feel good. Thanks to you.'

His eyes flicked to hers and his smile faltered. 'I was a little rough with you.'

Faith remembered the size of him and the gentle way he eased himself in as if he knew he'd be a tight fit. Then she remembered the way he lost control and thrust harder and harder until his head dropped and his body shook. Something hot and deep curled in her belly.

'Maybe I like it a little rough.'

He didn't smile. 'Really, are you all right?'

She moved her arm and propped her elbow up to rest her head on her hand. His eyes travelled down to her chest. Then he smiled and looked back.

'I've tackled meaner people than you and lived to tell the tale.'

'Who's been mean to you? Tell me where they live and I'll sort them out.'

Faith laughed and felt the comfort of his words even though she knew he was joking. To think that there was someone who was willing to stick up for her made her feel amazing but frightened all at once.

'They live back in England. Most of them. Probably mothers now with little girls of their own to train to push people around.'

He propped himself up on one arm and shot her a direct look. 'Girls at school were mean to you?'

Faith shrugged. 'It was boarding school. Everyone was mean to one another at some stage. You're away from home. You're sad. You're lonely. It takes its toll.'

Cash lifted a hand to push a strand of hair out of Faith's eyes and her breath hitched. His tenderness still surprised her and so did the look in his eyes. 'It doesn't make it right. I'm sorry that happened to you.'

'It's not your fault.'

'No, but I'm still sorry it happened. I'm sorry there were people who made you feel you weren't as brilliant and beautiful as you are.'

His tenderness made her stomach buzz. The feeling of pushing too hard and ruining everything bubbled up in her. She didn't want him to care for her like this. She didn't want his words to make her feel so cared for.

'It wasn't that bad,' she lied, looking away—knowing that if he saw her eyes he'd know the truth. He'd know that every day she was at school she felt sickening fear and horrible homesickness. She'd longed for a friend. She'd been desperate to get out, run away but she couldn't. She'd been trapped and lonely and sad. But that was over. That was her past. He was here now and he wasn't going anywhere. She looked back into his eyes. Or was he?

'So what now? You and me…what happens now?' It was then she saw it. Hesitation. A slight pause that ripped through her ferociously. Doubt. 'I mean…obviously…breakfast… what do you want? I make a mean blueberry pancake.' She moved away, meaning to get out. Away from the uncertainty in his eyes. Of course this wasn't going to last. Of course this was just a short-term thing.

'Faith, wait. There's something I have to tell you.'

And here it was. Faith's breathing became harder. She pulled away, out of his grasp, and reached for her dressing gown. She planted a smile on her face.

'You don't like pancakes?'

Cash sat up and the sheet fell away to reveal his mus- cled torso. She wanted to touch it. Touch him and lick him as she'd done last night. She wanted to feel his strong arms around her, pulling her close. Kissing her as if it were the last day on earth.

'I had a call from Gordon Grant yesterday afternoon. Before I came over.'

Faith's smile faded. She didn't want to talk about work; she wanted to know how he felt. She wanted to know what was going to happen next.

'He wants to keep your show on.'

Faith's throat dried up.

'He does?'

'Yes.' Cash's eyes didn't leave hers. 'But he wants you on the English station.'

Something cold washed over her. He wanted her to go back to England? A month ago this news would have given her all sorts of satisfaction. Being able to go home and show everyone that she'd made it? Put on the show the other sta- tions wouldn't touch? But right now, as Cash lay naked in her bed she didn't want to go anywhere. The only place she wanted to be was here.

'I don't know if that's a good idea.'

'Why not? It means you can keep your show on.' Cash

wasn't touching her. Caution fired her skin to stand on end. Why was he keeping his distance? Was this his 'get out of jail free' card? His way of getting rid of her without telling her? Was last night 'just sex' for him after all?

'Why didn't you tell me this last night?'

'I didn't want you to have to worry about it.'

'Worry about it? Why would I worry about it? It's all I've ever wanted. The chance to prove myself in the place that I couldn't get a start? Why would I worry about that?'

He'd known last night. Before they'd had sex. He'd known that this would end before it had a chance to begin.

'You don't have to go. I've decided to let you keep your show on here if you want.' Cash's eyes didn't display the warmth they had earlier today and it was making her feel frightened. What was he saying?

'You're keeping my show on?' Her voice came out as a squeak. No. Not this. Not again. Faith jumped up off the bed. Not now. Not after what they'd done. Please, don't let him be this man. She wasn't sure she could handle it if he were this man.

'If you want to stay.'

'And what then? Do we…do more of this? Is having sex with you part of the contract?'

'Faith. I thought we sorted all that out. I'm not offering you this so you'll sleep with me.'

'Yet you're offering me this just after you slept with me. Not before…' she held up a finger to him as she started pacing the room '…but after. When you knew what I'd do.'

'Faith…' Cash slid out of the bed, wrapping the sheet around his bottom half. He looked beautiful. Strong and solid and beautiful but what he was offering was anything but.

'No, don't say my name. You don't deserve to say my name. This was "just sex" for you, wasn't it?'

'No, it wasn't.'

'Liar. You are a liar. You knew about this. You knew Grant wanted me back in England but you didn't want me to go. Not until you finished with me anyway. Not until you used me up—then you could spit me out.'

'It's not like that…'

He reached for her but she pulled away from his hand. Satisfaction strangely settled over her. Relief rushed through her. Of course this would happen. She'd known it all along. It was too good to be true.

'Then what is it like? What do you want from me? Because I'll tell you what I want. More. More than just sex. I want you. I told you that. I told you I wanted more.'

Cash didn't move. He just looked at her and Faith felt the fear creep over her again. He knew what she wanted. This was his chance to tell her that he wanted her too. That he wanted her to stay with him—not because of the show but because he liked her. As much as she liked him. But he didn't.

CHAPTER TWENTY-SIX

CASH SWALLOWED. WHAT would she do? When Grant had contacted him yesterday afternoon he'd argued and fought and told the man he was making a mistake. He wanted Faith here. But then Grant had said something. That this was Faith's opportunity to get what she'd always wanted and he realised it was true. Doing her show in the UK would lead to much more than being a presenter on a local breakfast programme or even doing her show here. The Australian market was too small for any real success. And right then he'd realised he'd lost her before he'd even had a chance to have her.

'This is your chance, Faith. Your chance to have everything you ever wanted.' A shot of something painful passed through Cash's body when he said the words.

'I know. This *is* what I've always wanted.' She looked away. She didn't seem overly excited and that idea made his heart start to beat faster. Maybe she'd refuse. Maybe she'd want to stay. With him. Maybe she'd choose him.

'It means recognition. Awards.'

She shifted but didn't look at him so he looked away. The way she talked it was as if she was warming up to the idea. She was considering her options and he feared that he knew which way she was leaning. Another woman choosing something other than him. Nine years might have passed but it still felt the same. Like a rusty knife twisting in his guts.

'You'll have the career you always wanted.'

'Yes.'

Cash felt the bile rise to his throat. She'd made her choice. He'd stupidly thought that last night had meant something. That it was more than just sex. They'd connected. They'd seen each other. But when she looked back at him he knew. It had just been sex.

'So you're taking it?' he asked through gritted teeth.

Faith tried to tell him with her eyes. *Ask me to stay. Tell me you feel the way I do. Tell me that last night wasn't just sex. Please.*

'Yes. I have to take it. It's everything I've worked for.'

Cash nodded and she thought she saw something in his eyes. Something sad but it passed just as quickly as it had come.

'But thank you,' she said, her eyes not leaving his.

'What for?'

'For showing me what it feels like to be made love to.'

He didn't speak, he just watched her and she watched him until seconds turned into minutes and then he gathered his clothes from the floor where she'd flung them last night and held them in his arms.

'Your show is good, Faith. It just needs more direction. If you want me to, I can help you with it.'

The show. That was all this was about. That was all he wanted. Not her. It had never been her. And she'd had enough. He'd said she mattered; well, now it was time for him to prove it.

'Forget the show—I don't care about the show. I want to know what you have to offer me. You.'

He breathed deeply and his chest filled. She watched it before returning to his eyes. Those beautiful eyes that she was now sure she was in love with.

'I've told you what I can offer you.'

Faith nodded. Help with her show—that was what he was

offering her. That was all he'd meant when he'd said he was here for her. For the show. That was all.

'That's not enough for me.'

This time when Cash reached for her he wouldn't let her move away. He gripped her shoulders and made her look at him. He needed her to understand. He needed to tell her what he was thinking. Even if it was too honest. Even if she walked away and chose to leave, she had to know.

'Look at me, Faith. Listen to me.' She looked at him then and he saw her. Despite the way she jutted her chin out he knew he'd hurt her. She'd wanted more. 'I want you, Faith, but I can't fall for you...'

She looked away.

'Look at me.'

She turned back to meet his eyes. Defiantly. 'I know that.'

'It's not that I don't like you...'

'I don't want you to like me.'

'Or that I don't care about you...'

'I don't want you to care.'

'Faith, stop. Listen to me. Stop talking and listen.'

Her eyes finally met his. There were no tears there, just resolution. As if she'd finally accepted it. The way her blue eyes had turned soft was killing him.

'I can't fall for you. You don't understand. If I do...if I fall for you...I'll never recover.' And that was the truth. He couldn't let this mean anything more because he couldn't bear to have his heart broken all over again. He knew what she was going to choose; he knew it wouldn't be him and it hurt. It hurt like hell and all he wanted her to do was to deny it. To tell him that she chose him and that he was allowed to fall.

'I don't want you to fall for me, Cash. I want to go home and do my show.'

He let her go, watching her eyes the whole time. *Deny it,*

he screamed at her with his mouth shut. *Change your mind. Choose me.* But she didn't. So he gathered his clothes, got dressed and left.

CHAPTER TWENTY-SEVEN

FAITH HAD BEEN gone for three weeks, two days and seven hours and Cash hadn't managed to go any more than five minutes without thinking about her. The way she teased him. The way she wrapped herself around him when they made love. The way she looked at him the way she always did. As if they were speaking without saying a word. He missed her so much it hurt.

Even though he'd spent every spare minute surfing or running he was never tired enough to sleep through the night. She'd left. Without even a backward glance. Sex had become just sex and he couldn't help but feel disappointed. He'd expected more. He'd expected a fight or a tearful declaration of her love but…nothing. She'd packed her things and left to pursue her dreams. Without him. Rejection stung, but it hurt even more this time. This time there was more to it. She hadn't left him for anyone else—there was no one for him to hate. She'd just left, and somehow that felt infinitely worse.

His phone buzzed. He ignored it. Work had become just that lately. Work. All he wanted to do was get this station back on track and get back to the States. Escape to where he didn't have to think about any of this and where he could go back to being what he was. Numb. He wasn't even sure any more why he'd come home. Some part of him thought the reason he'd agreed to this had something to do with Charlie. Even before Faith had told him he shouldn't have given up on his relationship with his brother, he knew that his unfinished business was why he felt the way he did. Numb.

Numb until he met Faith. Until her touch made him feel again. When she'd kissed him the first time she'd told him she liked him. He'd thought she was trying to manipulate him. But she hadn't been. She'd been honest with him. From the start. She'd told him what she wanted. She hadn't hid her feelings. Even at the burlesque he knew what she wanted. He'd always thought he was the honest one but he realised now that he hadn't been honest from the start.

Faith was right. He'd been scared. Ever since Jess broke his foolish heart nine years ago. He'd been too scared to face his brother and too scared to stay on the farm and too scared to move on. Until Faith. Until she showed him what love was supposed to be like. Two people who cared about each other. Two people who didn't have sex—they made love.

Cash's phone buzzed again and he picked it up. Gordon Grant. Again. Faith's show had aired for the first time in the UK this week. He'd looked up the ratings. It had done well. It hadn't broken any records, but for a market that was usually famously conservative—she'd done extremely well.

'How are the ratings?' Gordon started the conversation as he did every other. 'Have we got any more advertisers?'

'No,' said Cash. 'They want more local content before committing.'

'That's not going to happen.'

Cash clenched his fist. Normally he'd be itching for this argument. He'd baffle Grant with the brilliance of his knowledge of rating and figures and programming and industry movements, but right now he couldn't give a stuff. He didn't want to think about TV. None of that was important. None of that mattered.

'How's Faith doing?'

Grant paused. 'Faith?'

Cash gritted his teeth. 'Yes, Faith. Faith Harris. Her new *Sexy London* show started over there this week.'

'Oh, the numbers weren't great. We're bringing in a co-median to co-host next week.'

'You're what?'

'Something like that. I'm not sure. It's not been a great earner for us to be honest and we've just heard a pitch for a new sports show that David Beckham's been linked to.'

Cash's blood hissed. 'You dragged her back over there to change the format on her? Then get rid of her?'

'That's the TV biz, Anderson—you know that.'

He knew that. He knew what a soul-sucking industry this was and he knew that eventually it would destroy Faith, the way it had almost destroyed him.

He'd spent the last nine years thinking it was OK to not speak to his brother. He'd spent the last nine years avoiding intimacy with anyone. Nine years thinking love didn't exist. But now he knew the truth and it had been Faith who'd taught him.

'I'll tell you what I know, Grant. Creating quality content is not about ratings and advertisers. It's about finding people who are passionate about what they do. It's about finding people who love what they do and letting them do it without interfering. By being there for them when they need it but allowing them to be themselves without thinking you know everything.'

Grant paused. 'Are you drunk, Anderson?'

Right then he did feel drunk, but then he supposed that was how love felt. It had been a long time since he felt it—but *drunk* did seem the right word to describe how he was feeling.

'If I am, I don't ever want to sober up.'

Without saying another word, Cash clicked off his call with Grant. There were only two calls he needed to make right now—one to his brother and the other to the airport.

He didn't want to be content. He wanted to fall—even if it meant he was going to get hurt; he wasn't scared any more.

'Do you have any idea how hard you are to track down?'

Faith had fallen asleep. The drinks she'd consumed at the station's Christmas party last night had allowed her brain to fuzz and she'd snuggled down into the warm sheets and drifted off. She'd cried herself to sleep last night, as she had almost every night for the past three weeks. She'd thought the ache in her chest would have eased by now but it was still there. Insistently knocking on her chest. Wanting to be let in.

She'd been dreaming when the knock sounded on the door and as she opened it the subject of her dreams—or nightmares, if she remembered the running and the calling and the falling and the crying—was there.

Scowling.

Dark look, dark suit and a dark heart.

Cash's eyebrows lowered. He moved his feet wider apart and pushed his hands in his pockets. Faith's sleepiness evaporated and her heart thumped in her chest. A slow procession of cold prickles raised up over her head. Was she still asleep? Him being here wasn't right. He looked out of place and she couldn't help thinking she'd manifested him here out of pure desire.

'Cash.' Faith's heart was beating so hard it was hurting. She wanted to touch him. To reach out and feel his skin and see if he was real. But she didn't. She stood still and looked at him with her mouth open.

It was him.

Here.

Standing at the door of her flat, waiting for her to say something else.

'What are you doing here?'

'I was in town and thought I'd look you up.'

Faith's heart stopped beating and her heart fell to the floor. 'Why?'

'I missed you.' She didn't miss the suggestion in his voice. She didn't miss the heat in his eyes. He was 'looking her up'. In other words—he wanted to have sex.

Fire heated her blood. How dared he? After everything. After the way he made love to her as if she meant something to him. After the way he held her and whispered into her hair. The way he slipped his fingers through hers and pulled her closer—kissing her forehead and her eyes before finally planting a tender kiss on her lips. The way he looked at her. Long looks that spoke of more than…just sex.

Faith gripped the door hard, then swung it as hard as she could.

But Cash was too quick. His foot slid into the door frame and the door swung open again.

'What are you doing here? Do you expect me to just lay down and let you have your way because you're here and you're horny? I'm not your tart.'

He pulled one hand out of his pocket and placed it on the door and she noticed his cheeks slash with colour.

'Then what are you, Faith? Because I'd like to know. What the hell are you to me?'

He was angry and the gruff way he spoke made Faith's stomach flip. His voice sounded raw, close to the edge. Emotional.

'We have nothing more to say to each other, Cash. We said everything when I was back home.'

'Right before you left?'

Faith noticed the vein in Cash's neck pop. It throbbed. His knuckles were white on the door. 'I had to leave. I was offered a job. You know that.'

'I know that.' He watched her eyes, one of his flicking to the other. The green slash in his left eye glinted.

'And I had to leave.'

He was silent. Faith let her eyes wander over him. His hair was longer. It curled a little at his ears. She wanted to run her hands through it. She wanted to put her palm on his cheek and let him rest in it. She wanted to take away that look in his eyes and massage his shoulders until they slumped. She wanted to make love to him.

Cash lifted a hand and touched the side of her mouth with the pad of his thumb. The heat from that small touch had her swaying towards him.

'You were drooling,' he said quietly.

Faith's hand flew up to her mouth to wipe away the dried saliva that pooled there. Heat flashed through her whole body. Drooling. Like a dog. Like a pathetic little puppy begging for a bone.

Enough.

'I don't need you to wipe up my drool, or come over here and have sex with me just because you're horny. I don't need you at all. I am perfectly happy to be on my own.'

He just looked at her.

'I love my job.'

He stepped closer.

'Cash…'

Her brain started to fog when a waft of his scent surrounded her. The memory of his warm skin and the way hers tingled when he kissed it wound through her brain. The gentleness of his touch and the pleasurable pain of his teeth as he nipped at her lips.

Enough.

'Stop.' She held her palm up to his chest, not quite touching it and willing him not to touch her. She didn't know what she'd do if he actually touched her. 'You need to go.'

He didn't move and the nervous fluttering inside her grew. 'What do you want from me? What do you want?'

Deep down she knew she wanted him to say 'you'. She wanted him to ask her to come home. She wanted him to say she was his and he was hers and that they had to be together. But he didn't say 'you'. His smile faltered.

'Can I come in?'

'No.'

'We need to talk.'

'So talk.'

'Here? In the hallway?'

'Wait here.'

Cash's jaw clamped shut and a twitch in his jaw started to jump. He looked...angry and frustrated and about ready to walk away. What did he want? Just sex...or something else?

As she shut the door on him she had to tell herself to breathe. Of course he just wanted sex. Why else would he be here? She was an idiot to think he was here to spend time with her or—God forbid—tell her he'd made a mistake and she was the most important thing in the world to him and that he wanted to wrap her in his arms and take her away from all this—take her home.

She let out a huff of laughter as she pulled on some jeans and located her boots, slipping them on over her thick woollen socks. If Cash wanted her he would have said something by now. No—he was here for sex. Just sex. And it was time to tell him the truth. She didn't want to have sex with him—not now—not ever. She wanted more.

CHAPTER TWENTY-EIGHT

WHEN SHE WAS wrapped in her scarf and coat, had her woolly gloves and knee-high boots on, Faith opened the door to find Cash leaning up against the wall, waiting for her. When he turned his head to look at her, her breath caught. He was gorgeous. His dark eyes held her steady and a layer of stubble had spread across his jaw where the collar of his grey wool coat met his neck. She wanted to reach out and touch him. Feel the strength of the muscles in his shoulders and the ironic softness of his full, pale lips. His eyes softened and slid over her face, making her shiver. What was he thinking about? Would he be thinking about the last time they were together?

Because she was.

Every touch, every taste, every sound.

She still wanted him. Or at least her body did. Even if he didn't love her. Even if he was going to hurt her. Which was exactly why she should stay away from him. He pushed off from the wall and his big body faced her.

'Ready?'

She felt small. Childlike. As if he could lift his arms and wrap her up and make everything better. But she wasn't a child. She was a grown woman. And she didn't need his help. She didn't need him. She drew herself up and took a step back.

'Yes.' She started towards the lifts, then changed her

mind. She didn't want to be in such a small space with him and this lift had a tendency to break down. Instead she headed for the stairs. She didn't even stop to see if he was following but she knew he was. She could feel him behind her. She went as fast as was safely possible and when she arrived in the foyer with its peeling paint and slightly manky smell she moved as quickly as she could to the door.

She was grateful for the bracing chill and the layer of early morning darkness. Pulling her scarf tighter, she started to walk, only to be stopped by Cash's hand wrapped around her arm. His touch burned through her heavy coat and her woollen jumper as well as her long-sleeved shirt to her skin beneath. He had an uncanny way of finding her skin and getting underneath it.

'This way,' he growled in her ear.

He let go and turned in the opposite direction to disappear down a narrow laneway. She had no other option than to follow. The laneway was dark and intimate and perfect for a private kiss, she thought, before shaking that thought away. She had to tell herself to breathe again as she scurried on the wet cobblestones to keep up with his long strides. He walked and walked without a word. What was going on? Where was he taking her? Was something wrong? What did he want?

Finally he stopped. He pulled her around the corner of the laneway into a tiny, dark alley and gently pushed her back against the wall.

'Cash, what's going on? What's wrong? What are we doing here?'

'I need to talk to you and I don't want any interruptions.'

She looked up into his face as his eyes flashed with anger. A shiver escaped down her spine and it had nothing to do with the cold.

'What's happened? Is something wrong?' A horrible thought settled over her. A feeling of being at the side of that bridge, except this time Cash wasn't holding her. His hand was right there but she couldn't grab hold.

His look was hard for a second, then it gentled. He moved closer until she could feel his warm breath on her face. She couldn't help it; she instinctively reached for his warm body. Her fingers dragged the lapels of his coat closer and he responded by pushing his hard chest and his hips against her and putting his hands on the wall behind her head.

She drew in a long breath of the cool air. He fitted over her body perfectly. The hard planes of his body were like a casing for her and she closed her eyes and remembered. She remembered the way he breathed and the way he moaned deep in his throat when he was close. She remembered the feel of his fingers, a little rough as they tickled her skin. She remembered the feel of his lips and the feel of his tongue as he explored and kissed and licked her everywhere...

Her eyes sprang open. Something was different. Cash was wild. Like an animal. Primal. Possessive. And his mouth was slightly open. She was very much in danger of letting him in again. She was practically giving him the razor and telling him to cut her open. Her heart was beating so hard she was sure he could feel it through the layers of his clothes. He wanted her; she could see it. She could feel it.

Yet he didn't want her.

He was playing with her, tempting her. Giving her a taste of something she could never have. The only sounds were their mingled breaths and the heat of them made puffs of air escape from between their bodies. She wanted to kiss him. Wanted to let him have whatever he wanted. But instead she pushed him away.

'What are you doing here, Cash? What do you want from me? How much more can I give?'

He stumbled a little at her push, as if he was surprised she'd done it. His hands went back into his pockets.

'You left, remember? Not me.'

'I left because I had to. Because this job is everything I've ever wanted.'

'That's why you left?' He stared but didn't come closer.

'No. Yes.' Faith was confused. That wasn't why she left. 'I left because you cancelled my show.'

'That's not why you left.'

It wasn't why she left, but she didn't want him to know the real reason. She couldn't bear the thought that he would know. Know how she felt. Know that she loved him. Sucking in a breath, she tried to think.

'Of course it is.'

'No, it's not.'

'Then why? Why did I leave?'

'Because I hurt you.'

Faith stilled. He had hurt her. He was hurting her now. The cold air that she sucked in got caught in her lungs. It burned. It hurt.

'Yes.' Her voice had gone quiet. Her shoulders slumped and she felt weak. As if he'd stripped all the bones from her body and her skin was all that was holding her up. 'You hurt me.'

He didn't say anything, just held her eyes with his. Holding her up. Holding her steady as he had that day at the back of his wagon.

'I wanted more than just sex. I wanted you. I wanted you to feel the same about me that I felt about you,' she said.

Faith's heart hurt with the weight of each slow beat. She didn't take her eyes off his. They weren't touching but his eyes still seemed to be the only thing holding her up.

'What about now? Do you want to be with me now?' His voice sounded a little desperate and Faith felt a sudden and irrational surge of warmth. Hope. That was what surged through her. Irrational hope that maybe he wanted more than just sex too. But she knew that was stupid. He'd let her walk away and hadn't stopped her.

'I want someone to love me.'

Cash breathed out heavily. 'You left. You walked away. You chose this and I respect that, but I still have this ridiculous need to tell you how I feel about you.'

How he felt about her? The beating in her chest got louder, and harder.

He let out a breath and stepped back. Enough to rest his back on the wall behind him. He was two feet away yet it felt like miles.

'Faith, you are...' His direct look hit her.

'I am what?'

'You are...' She could see he was struggling with words. He was about to tell her how he felt about her. And she feared it wasn't what she wanted.

'What? A distraction? A good sport? What am I, Cash?'

She turned to go; she didn't want to feel this. He'd already broken her heart once and she didn't want him to do it again. Not him. All she wanted to do was run far away from the tsunami of pain that was heading her way. But he was too quick. His arm on hers stopped her and he pushed her back against the wall.

'Faith, stop. Stop running. Stop thinking everyone is going to hurt you. Stop thinking you don't deserve to be loved, because you do.'

Hot tears teased her eyes. She was confused and angry and upset and embarrassed and she didn't know what to say or what to do, but the warmth of his hand on her arm was calming her and she needed it to stay there.

'You don't have to be alone any more. You don't have to do it all on your own. I'm here for you.'

Time stopped. Faith's throat dried up.

'I want you, Faith—no. I need you. And I think you need me too.'

His voice was raw. She looked into his eyes and saw the emotion there. The pain, the hurt, the confusion.

'Cash, what are you talking about? You said sex was just sex.'

'Sex is not just sex. Sex is so much more than that,' he said gruffly, pushing her back against the wall. His eyes were close, and his breath was hot on her neck. 'So much more.'

It was more than that. His dark eyes locked with hers. She wanted to reach up and rub her hand along his rough stubble. She wanted to draw his face down into a comforting kiss. She wanted to take what he was offering. But she couldn't. Because she knew she couldn't do this.

'I can't, Cash,' she whispered, not wanting to say the words but knowing she needed to anyway. Because she couldn't bear it if he changed his mind. She'd fallen too far to be able to find her way back.

Cash's eyes flicked to her mouth, then back to her eyes, and his brow furrowed. His eyes moved back to her mouth. He looked as if he didn't understand what she was saying.

'You don't want me?'

Faith could feel his desperation deep in her chest. She wanted to give in. But she knew him too well; she knew that he was scared. Scared to trust her and scared to let her get too close.

'The only way you can really love someone is to trust them. To give yourself over to them completely. You can't hold back just in case you might get hurt and I don't know if you are capable of giving me that much.' Faith could hear the resignation in her voice. 'I don't know if you want it enough.'

Faith struggled to go on. He wasn't saying anything. He was just watching her. She couldn't figure out what he was thinking and she felt worse than she'd ever felt in her life. Worse than when everyone had found out about Mr Turner. Worse than when she was turned down at her local station for her show. Worse than when Cash had told her he didn't like her. She felt completely alone. But he'd said she wasn't alone. He'd said he needed her.

'Tell me you don't want this, and I'll leave you alone. Tell me you don't want to be with me.'

Cash's eyes flashed angrily and he stepped towards her. 'Do you have any idea what you've done to me? I've spent the last nine years thinking I knew exactly what I was doing but as soon as I met you I realised I had no idea.'

Faith stilled.

He came towards her with a force she wasn't expecting. He grabbed her arms and she looked up into his eyes. He was hurting; she could see that. He was struggling to understand how he felt and was struggling to let her go.

'You made me realise that I don't know anything. Sex isn't about power. It's about revealing yourself, being completely vulnerable. It's about trusting someone completely.'

Cash looked wild and desperate and out of his depth and she'd never seen him like that. As if he felt something more. Something raw and desperate. Love.

Moving closer, she lifted her hands to rest on his chest. He swayed towards her but she pulled back and kept her eyes on his. Those dark eyes were hard to resist. She wanted to kiss him, she wanted to tell him how she felt, but she needed him to say it first. She needed him to love her all on his own, without any prompting. Because if he loved her, that changed everything.

He tilted his head, his eyes moving from her eyes to her lips. She moved with him, their bodies moving together. Her palm slipped up to feel the roughness of his jaw and he put his hand over hers. Still she watched his eyes and when they flicked back to hers she knew that he knew.

'I trust you, Faith. I trust you and I need you.'

His other arm came around her waist and held her to him. They stopped moving. They held fast and his eyes were back on hers.

'I need you and you need me.'

His voice was not much more than a whisper. Faith felt as if she were teetering on the edge of that bridge. It was time. Time to close her eyes and jump. And it might hurt when she hit the bottom, but she realised that it didn't matter. That free-fall into the unknown—for a time when everything was perfect, it was worth it. She wanted to jump. With him. Faith smiled gently before raising herself up on her toes and kissing him gently on his slightly parted lips.

'Cash? I need to know. Do you love me?'

He responded by pressing his mouth tenderly to hers. His lips shook beneath hers as his hand snaked up her waist and rested on her cheek. Faith felt his kiss. She could feel his affection and she knew he felt as much as she did. They stood with their foreheads touching for too long. Faith's chest heaved and she knew that somewhere deep inside her swelling chest her heart was twisting. Her dream was twisting.

'With every breath in my body.' His voice was deep and she felt it rumble against her chest.

Faith held her breath. All thoughts left her head. Her show, her doubt, everything. Except him and his voice and the flash of green in his eye. His eyes had become so familiar to her she couldn't bear the thought of not seeing them ever again.

'Are you all right?' he asked. Concern, worry. That was what swam in his eyes. And something else. Something she'd been dreaming of ever since that first kiss.

'Yes, now. Now everything's all right,' she whispered.

She couldn't say anything else for a moment as her eyes met his. But the look in his eyes didn't change. His hands dropped down her body to rest on her hips.

'I came here for one reason. You. I want you. I need you.'

Faith noticed the strain in his gruff voice.

'You can walk away from this if you want. You can leave, but it won't matter. It was never just sex with you. Never.' His eyes had locked with hers and he wasn't letting go. They were sincere and burning dark. Faith had never felt so safe yet so in danger in her life. 'And I love you. And I want to spend the rest of my life loving you,' he added with one of his wicked grins.

A smile twitched at Faith's mouth as her heart swelled painfully.

'I told you I knew what I was talking about.'

He smiled and pulled her even closer. Faith ran the back of her hand across the beginnings of stubble on his cheek. When her knuckles met his mouth he kissed them, his eyes on hers. He smiled with his lips still on her knuckles and raised one incredibly sexy eyebrow.

Faith's stomach flipped.

When their lips met, Faith felt her body fall as it melted into his. But when his strong arms came around her back he lifted her feet off the ground and kissed her long and hard and deep. He was strong and smelled so good and Faith could hardly remember to breathe. And then he set her down and let her go and the whip of the cool night air circled her shoulders. 'I have never felt more in danger of falling off that bridge than I do now,' she whispered.

Cash chuckled and stood, taking her hands in his.

'You're not in danger, you're in love. And you shouldn't fall, you should jump.'

'I'm jumping. With no parachute,' she said with a smile.

'I'll be your parachute.' He lifted her off her feet and pressed his mouth tenderly to hers. She moved against him and shivered as his tongue slid against her lips.

'Does this mean we can go home and have "just sex"?' she whispered.

He opened his eyes and looked directly into hers. Hot and dark and deep. 'No. I want to make love. Hot, hard, wild love,' he said, his voice gruff.

'Good, because I'm not very good at sex.'

He smiled and his eyes crinkled at the side. 'Oh, yes, you bloody are.' This time his kiss was passionate and deep and he nipped at her lips. When they drew away to breathe, Faith smiled and snuggled into the crook of his arm. Safe. Warm. Right where she belonged.

'You're not too bad yourself.'

* * * * *

Mills & Boon® Hardback
May 2014

ROMANCE

The Only Woman to Defy Him	Carol Marinelli
Secrets of a Ruthless Tycoon	Cathy Williams
Gambling with the Crown	Lynn Raye Harris
The Forbidden Touch of Sanguardo	Julia James
One Night to Risk it All	Maisey Yates
A Clash with Cannavaro	Elizabeth Power
The Truth About De Campo	Jennifer Hayward
Sheikh's Scandal	Lucy Monroe
Beach Bar Baby	Heidi Rice
Sex, Lies & Her Impossible Boss	Jennifer Rae
Lessons in Rule-Breaking	Christy McKellen
Twelve Hours of Temptation	Shoma Narayanan
Expecting the Prince's Baby	Rebecca Winters
The Millionaire's Homecoming	Cara Colter
The Heir of the Castle	Scarlet Wilson
Swept Away by the Tycoon	Barbara Wallace
Return of Dr Maguire	Judy Campbell
Heatherdale's Shy Nurse	Abigail Gordon

MEDICAL

200 Harley Street: The Proud Italian	Alison Roberts
200 Harley Street: American Surgeon in London	Lynne Marshall
A Mother's Secret	Scarlet Wilson
Saving His Little Miracle	Jennifer Taylor

Mills & Boon® Large Print

May 2014

ROMANCE

HISTORICAL

MEDICAL

ROMANCE

Ravelli's Defiant Bride	Lynne Graham
When Da Silva Breaks the Rules	Abby Green
The Heartbreaker Prince	Kim Lawrence
The Man She Can't Forget	Maggie Cox
A Question of Honour	Kate Walker
What the Greek Can't Resist	Maya Blake
An Heir to Bind Them	Dani Collins
Playboy's Lesson	Melanie Milburne
Don't Tell the Wedding Planner	Aimee Carson
The Best Man for the Job	Lucy King
Falling for Her Rival	Jackie Braun
More than a Fling?	Joss Wood
Becoming the Prince's Wife	Rebecca Winters
Nine Months to Change His Life	Marion Lennox
Taming Her Italian Boss	Fiona Harper
Summer with the Millionaire	Jessica Gilmore
Back in Her Husband's Arms	Susanne Hampton
Wedding at Sunday Creek	Leah Martyn

MEDICAL

200 Harley Street: The Soldier Prince	Kate Hardy
200 Harley Street: The Enigmatic Surgeon	Annie Claydon
A Father for Her Baby	Sue MacKay
The Midwife's Son	Sue MacKay

Mills & Boon® Large Print
June 2014

ROMANCE

A Bargain with the Enemy	Carole Mortimer
A Secret Until Now	Kim Lawrence
Shamed in the Sands	Sharon Kendrick
Seduction Never Lies	Sara Craven
When Falcone's World Stops Turning	Abby Green
Securing the Greek's Legacy	Julia James
An Exquisite Challenge	Jennifer Hayward
Trouble on Her Doorstep	Nina Harrington
Heiress on the Run	Sophie Pembroke
The Summer They Never Forgot	Kandy Shepherd
Daring to Trust the Boss	Susan Meier

HISTORICAL

Portrait of a Scandal	Annie Burrows
Drawn to Lord Ravenscar	Anne Herries
Lady Beneath the Veil	Sarah Mallory
To Tempt a Viking	Michelle Willingham
Mistress Masquerade	Juliet Landon

MEDICAL

From Venice with Love	Alison Roberts
Christmas with Her Ex	Fiona McArthur
After the Christmas Party...	Janice Lynn
Her Mistletoe Wish	Lucy Clark
Date with a Surgeon Prince	Meredith Webber
Once Upon a Christmas Night...	Annie Claydon

0514 GEN STD LP

Discover more romance at

www.millsandboon.co.uk

- ❤ WIN great prizes in our exclusive competitions
- ❤ BUY new titles before they hit the shops
- ❤ BROWSE new books and REVIEW your favourites
- ❤ SAVE on new books with the Mills & Boon® Bookclub™
- ❤ DISCOVER new authors

PLUS, to chat about your favourite reads, get the latest news and find special offers:

 Find us on facebook.com/millsandboon

🐦 Follow us on twitter.com/millsandboonuk

❤ Sign up to our newsletter at millsandboon.co.uk